THE GOLD-PLATED
SEWER

Also by Ovid Demaris

Ride The Gold Mare
The Hoods Take Over
The Lusting Drive
The Long Night
The Slasher
The Extortioners
The Enforcer
The Gold-Plated Sewer
Candyleg aka Machine Gun McCain
The Parasite
The Organization aka The Contract)
Fatal Mistake
Mason's Women
The Overlord
Legs Diamond
The Vegas Legacy
Ricochet

THE GOLD-PLATED SEWER

OVID DEMARIS

CUTTING EDGE

ISBN-13: 978-1-952138-42-3

Published by
Cutting Edge Publishing
PO Box 8212
Calabasas, CA 91372
www.cuttingedgebooks.com

1

I T WAS a warm, brilliant, smogless spring day and I had the top down. Ahead lay the pink stucco walls and hangarlike sound stages of Goldman Studios—the prosaic façade of a jaded wonderland. I brought the Ford to a full stop before the watchman's gatehouse and waited while he chatted leisurely on the phone. He had given me one sharp appraising look and decided I could wait. I didn't mind waiting. The radio was on and Basie was swinging.

Five minutes later, he hung up, hitched up his gun belt and sauntered over to the car, placing a beefy hand on the side mirror.

"Yeah," he said, ready for an argument. "No tourists allowed on the lot. Gotta have a pass."

"How about an appointment with old Harry?" I said. "Does he carry any weight with you?"

The hand came off the mirror and the pudgy body stiffened to attention. "You mean Mr. Goldman, sir?" He damn near saluted.

"That's the one."

"Yes, sir. May I have your name, sir?"

"Slader. Vince Slader."

He scurried into the gatehouse, quickly checked a clipboard hanging by the phone and scurried right back out again.

"Sorry to have kept you waiting, sir," he said. "That was a business call I had back there."

"Sure," I said. "Don't worry about it. Where do I go from here?"

He gave me a painfully sincere smile. "Thank you, sir. Just follow that yellow line. It leads right to the administration building. Mr. Goldman's office is on the fourth floor. Room four-oh-two."

I nodded and drove away before he had a chance to try that salute again. I took it easy on the accelerator. The street was narrow and the place was buzzing with activity, and I didn't want to damage any of those expensive properties sashaying around in brief shorts and tight sweaters. It all looked so young and tender. This kind of stuff gets to looking better every year, and at forty-one it looks damn delicious.

There was a flagpole in front of the administration building, and Old Glory was flapping as jauntily as a starlet. I drove into a parking slot that said *Reserved for Executive Personnel.*

I found room 402 easily enough. Gold block letters announced that it was PRIVATE. I opened the door and peeked in. Four beautiful pairs of eyes looked up from typewriter keyboards and turned in my direction. I quickly passed my smile around.

"Just looking for Harry."

"Mr. Slader?"

"That's me," I said, approaching the blonde at the head of typewriter row.

"Will you please have a seat?"

I ignored the innuendo and took a chair facing them. If I ever decide to become an executive, this is the place for me. The blonde spoke into an inter-office phone and stood up.

"Will you come with me, sir?" This dame was full of meaty suggestions.

The next office was larger and had only one secretary. It was easy enough to see why she had jumped to the head of the class. She was tall and statuesque, with coppery hair and deep blue eyes as sharp as they were pretty.

"You're late, Mr. Slader. Mr. Goldman had to take another appointment ahead of you. His schedule is very crowded today. I am afraid you will have to wait now."

"Sorry to be late," I said lamely. Her brusque, efficient manner made me feel like a delinquent schoolboy. Unfortunately, dames like her leave me as they take me. Cold.

I went and sat down in a blue leather chair, and she went and sat behind her blue steel desk. I looked down to see what she did with those long legs and found my view blocked by a modesty panel. I suppose that's the business world's equivalent of the chastity belt. What you don't see during working hours won't give you any time-consuming dirty ideas.

I folded my arms and stared out across the top of her copper head at the top of a balding palm tree, gently swaying in the spring breeze. She kept damn busy answering the telephone. Each time she picked up the receiver, she removed her earring. Slowly, I became intrigued by her coldly affected mannerisms. Hell, it was afternoon and dragging time for me, and still this dame looked like she had just stepped out of her morning shower. Every hair in place, clothes fresh and unwrinkled, make-up on straight, not a tired muscle anywhere. She was too much.

The minutes lengthened into half an hour and I started to get restless. I scooted down lower in the chair, and she glanced sharply at me. I straightened up slightly and smiled.

"Sorry, teach," I said. "Got carried away there for a minute."

She didn't crack a smile. I guess being in the front office of a movie studio had conditioned her to characters.

"How much longer is Harry going to take?" I asked, standing up and walking to the window behind her desk. "It's a beautiful day for golf. You play golf?"

She turned her head without moving her body. "Do I impress you as the athletic type?" she said. It wasn't exactly a question the way she put it.

I looked her over closely, moving away from the window to get a better view of that statuesque figure. "You're big enough to be a good one."

She turned her head and started shuffling papers, ignoring me completely. I returned my gaze to the window. A flat-bottom trailer truck was hauling the façade walls of a southern mansion. Messenger girls sped by on bicycles, their brown legs glistening in the sunlight. Expensive sports cars and Cadillac convertibles vied for attention.

A buzzer sounded behind me, and I heard Miss Efficiency stand up.

"Mr. Goldman will see you now," she said, walking to the door ahead of me.

Harry Goldman sat behind his monstrous desk like the movie version of a movie mogul. He was a short, paunchy man with a soft pink face and pure-white closely cropped hair. His bulbous nose was as blue as a summer sky.

"This is Mr. Slader," she said.

"I know, I know," he said, nodding at me. He remained seated. "I've got to see Meyer's rushes at three. Buzz me."

"Yes, sir," she said, backing out of the office, quickly closing the door on her fading smile.

"Sit down," Goldman said, pointing to a leather chair facing his desk.

I sat down and he towered above me. That swivel chair must have been jacked up to infinity.

"Slader," he said, rubbing fat stubby fingers across layers of pink chins. "I don't have any time to waste. I'm a very busy man. I've got pictures shooting all over the place. Big budget pictures and big stars who need big help all the time. I've got to be available to give them that help..."

This wasn't my first experience with movie people. I knew, for instance, that it's strictly routine for any of these characters to spend the first fifteen minutes on personal fluff. Everybody here is always turned *on*. It doesn't matter whether or not you're buying, they're still out there selling.

I half listened as I let my eyes travel over the office. It was an enormous room with a minimum of furniture, creating an illusion of even greater space. The room was painted in one of those soft cream colors, something like a rose beige, and the color scheme was carried out in the furnishings, drapes and carpeting. There was the usual casting couch, this one about twelve feet long, with an equally long coffee table before it loaded down with books and magazines. One solid wall was all glass, with a gossamer drape drawn over it, giving the room a soft subdued pink glow. But the main piece of furniture, the focal point, was the desk, a big old English antique dating back no doubt to the Middle Ages. It had probably belonged to Richard the Lion-Hearted. The idea quickly depressed me.

"...that's the only reason I'm here. A lot of my darling girls and boys call me Papa. They consider me with the same high respect and deep affection. I am like their own flesh-and-blood fathers. It's a wonderful relationship. I am proud of it. I am the big papa and they are my little children. And, like their big papa, I wipe their noses, hold their hands, give them money and fame. I keep them happy."

I had to look away.

He noticed my wandering look and abruptly stopped talking. He looked at his wrist watch, tapping it with one finger. "See, at most, I can give you ten minutes. Maybe fifteen if positively necessary. I've got enough work here to keep ten men busy as bees all day long. Twenty-four hours a day. This job is gonna put me in my grave ten years ahead of my time."

He was pushing seventy-five and looked healthy enough to rock-and-roll through the next quarter century.

"Slader. I need a man I can trust. A man who can keep his big mouth shut. I don't need no blabbermouth. You understand what I mean? I want this to be a privileged conversation. Just like a lawyer or doctor. Better still, like a priest. Do I make myself positively clear?"

OVID DEMARIS

"Positively," I said.

"Good, good. Milner tells me you're a private eye. What I need right now is a clam. Somebody who can keep his lip buttoned up one hundred per cent tight. We're in the middle of shooting *Run for Home* and it goes out on location Monday. We're flying the whole cast to Kansas on Sunday. We can't afford to have anything go wrong. Get it?"

I shook my head. "No."

He threw himself forward in his highchair and punched the buzzer on the inter-office phone. "Send Gus in right away," he said.

Gus Milner did not waste any of Papa's precious time. He made it in seven seconds flat. After introductions, he started pacing around my chair, his hands behind his back, his thin gray face contorting nervously. Milner was a little fellow, not more than five-five or six, and very skinny and dry-looking. His head was bald and pointed, with only a fringe of curly gray hair, reminding me of the halo of a trappist monk. He had a long, curved nose, razor-sharp at the tip. The nostrils quivered each time his lips moved. After a while his hand came up and pinched the nostrils with thumb and forefinger, holding them while he continued to talk in a nasal twang.

Goldman interrupted him before he had a chance to become coherent. It was quite clear that Harry did not allow competition. Milner sat down in a leather chair next to mine and nodded to punctuate Goldman's oratory. He never stopped smiling. It made me tired just to look at those straining facial muscles.

A buzzer sounded and Goldman glanced at his watch. "I've got two minutes, that's all. Meyer's rushes need my personal attention."

"Look, H.G., you go ahead. I'll brief Slader and take him over to the house."

Goldman ran his chubby hands through his white hair, biting on his lower lip. "Good, good," he said. "But Gus, for God's

6

sake, don't antagonize Freddie. I'm the one who has to listen to his tantrums. I don't have time for any more fits. I'm a busy man."

"Now wait a minute, H.G. I'm his personal manager. I can handle him."

"Why don't you do it then? Why bring me all those problems? I've got problems of my own. You want to see some problems? I've got a bushel full right there in front of your nose. Involves millions of dollars. Every one of them a crisis. Sometimes I wish I was a stock boy. No more problems. Live the good life. Nobody after you all the time to do this and that and every other crazy thing. I'm tired, Gus. I don't want any more problems. Now, you tell that to Freddie. I'm just gonna put my foot down. I'm just too easy..."

I stopped listening to Harry's sad tale. I'm afraid I couldn't sympathize with his problem. People took about as much advantage of him as they had of Genghis Khan. Then suddenly I heard the words "death threat" and the name "Sharpe." I looked up at Goldman. He was staring at me, his small eyes waiting for my reaction.

"Do you have those letters here?"

"Yes. They're in my safe," he said. "They were addressed to me."

"How many were there?"

"Three. All said exactly the same thing."

"Can I see them?"

He spoke to Miss Efficiency on the intercom, and a moment later she hurried into the room with a brown Manila envelope. Goldman opened it and handed me three white envelopes. I noticed that they all had been postmarked in Beverly Hills at two-day intervals. Inside each I found a three-by-four file card. Nothing had been written on the cards. Instead, the sender had clipped the words from newspapers and pasted them on the cards—a fairly typical procedure in such cases. And foolproof as far as tracing it was concerned. The message consisted of only ten words: *Freddie Sharpe will die before* Run for Home *is finished.*

"What do you think?" Milner asked.

I replaced the cards in their respective envelopes and handed them back to Goldman. "Could be a crackpot," I said. "It doesn't sound like a psycho. They usually indulge in more violent threats, with a fair sprinkling of obscene language. This is quite mild."

"Is that all?" Goldman asked. "Aren't there any clues you can follow to find this man ?"

I smiled. "I only saw the same things you did."

"Well, by God, he can't die before the picture is finished. You know what that could mean? A five-million-dollar budget gone down the drain."

Milner jumped up. "H.G.! I'm ashamed of you. How about poor Freddie? He's worth a lot more than a lousy five-million budget."

"You're ashamed of me?" Goldman whispered hoarsely. "You said the wrong thing that time. After all I've done for Freddie. And you. Let me tell you something. There are lots of executives in this studio who are fed up with Freddie Sharpe. They are in here all the time complaining. 'Too hard to handle,' they say. 'He's not worth all the headaches.' If they had their way Freddie wouldn't be starring in *Run for Home*. I'm the one who fought for him. I'm the one who is like a father to that boy. I've done more for him than I would have for my own flesh and blood. I've protected him from his enemies. Hundreds of enemies." His voice had started to rise, and the pink cheeks were turning a fiery red. "I had to fire sixteen—no, eighteen—people last year just to please him. Prop men, grips, messenger girls. Every day he had a new name for me to can. I don't like that. It's not nice. Freddie has got to learn to live with people…"

I had heard of Freddie Sharpe, all right. Who hadn't? This guy had been an institution on the front pages since the War. He had started out as a singer, the teaser kind, drooling out sexy words and sounds, half bent over a microphone, while millions of sex-starved teen-agers cheered and cried and swooned, all making it vicariously.

Gradually, as the years passed, a change in voice and style brought a change in audience. Without a loss in popularity he deftly shifted camps, trading in the kids for the parents. Went from six-bit singles to five-buck albums. From there he crashed the movies, first musicals, then suddenly into a straight dramatic role and immediate success. Overnight, he became the most sought-after actor in Hollywood. A Freddie Sharpe picture was a sure bet to gross a fat profit. Every producer in town was after him, ready and willing to give him a percentage of any property he selected. Freddie Sharpe was a Big Man in the entertainment business. Big enough to make Harry Goldman sweat gold.

I interrupted H.G. "Have you notified the police?"

Goldman glared at me. "Of course not. We don't want the police. Freddie has a mania about publicity. He doesn't want any of it concerning his private life. This has to be kept out of the newspapers."

"Yeah," Milner said. "And, besides, we're leaving for Kansas on Monday. The cops here can't do us any good. And the hick town we're going to wouldn't know which end was up. We need somebody to stay with Freddie twenty-four hours a day. We need good solid protection. Somebody to be around in case this crackpot happens to be serious. We don't want to take any chances, but we don't want to get splashed all over the front page, either. Freddie would really blow his lid. And I'm not kidding."

I scratched the top of my scalp. "Who in hell is this guy? Dracula?"

It was Milner's turn to glare at me. It was plain that I wasn't making a very good first impression. "Freddie is a sweet boy. The sweetest. Sure, he's temperamental. Why not? He's an artist. He's not like you and me. He's got a soul. A real sensitive soul. This man feels life in every nerve in his body. And I'll tell you something else, too. I've never met a man with a bigger, more generous heart. Right, H.G.?"

"That's positively right," Goldman said, his pink face suddenly beaming with love. "Freddie is a sweet, generous boy. There's nothing I wouldn't do for Freddie. That boy has a personality. I mean he's electric. When he smiles, the whole world lights up. I've known a lot of great talent in my time. Fifty years in the movie business, thank the Lord, and I've never met a greater talent than Freddie Sharpe. That boy could be the greatest actor of the century if he really applied himself. There's nothing he couldn't do if he really put his mind to it. He sings like a nightingale. Oh, how he can sing. He can act, too. He can read a script once and assimilate the characterization just like that"—and he snapped his stubby manicured fingers. "I've never known anyone like him."

"It's all right," I said. "You don't have to sell him to me. I'm not producing anything this year."

"This is not a joking matter," Milner said. "Freddie is the most important property in show business today. We need protection. H.G. had you checked out, and you're the man for the job. What do you say?"

"I don't think so," I said. "It looks like a full-time job. It would take me out of circulation for too long a period. And, besides, I don't feel like going to Kansas. I've been there before."

"What's your usual fee?" Goldman asked.

"Hundred a day, plus expenses."

He rubbed his chins again, his small eyes narrowing in deep concentration. "Pay you a thousand a week, plus all expenses. And don't forget. You'll have fun. Around with movie stars all the time. Maybe you'll even get yourself a little high-class nookie on the side. Gus will introduce you to Lisa Love. She co-stars with Freddie in *Run for Home*. Sweet girl. You'll love Lisa."

That did it. I don't know if it was the grand a week or the high-class nookie on the side. In any case, it was an unbeatable parlay.

2

A FTER A few thousand more irrelevant words by the busy Mr. Goldman, Gus Milner offered to drive me to my new home.

"You'll love Freddie," he said when we reached the parking lot. "He's the sweetest guy on earth."

As far as I was concerned, I was going to save my love for Lisa. I had been to a number of her movies and I'd liked what I'd seen.

We got into his Cadillac and drove off in the direction of Beverly Hills.

"Don't worry about your car," he said. "I've already arranged for somebody to drive it up to Freddie's. It'll be there when we arrive. What did you think of H.G.?"

"Great little worker," I said. "Busy as ten little bees twenty-four hours a day."

"He's okay. Bad guy to cross, if you know what I mean. But if you're square with him, H.G. can be okay."

"What about all those enemies? Any chance one of them could be after Freddie's blood for real? I mean something besides the usual Hollywood stuff."

"Look," Milner said. "Maybe I should wise you up right now. I don't want any misunderstanding. Freddie is a sweet guy. Do anything for a pal. I mean that. I sincerely mean every word of it. But once in a while he flips his lid and somebody gets hurt. Well, that's show business. When a guy is as big as Freddie, he can't turn around without making enemies. Hell, you beat somebody out of a role and bingo—you've made an enemy. You fire some-body for goofing off, bingo—another enemy. Who the hell can keep count? A guy in Freddie's position has to be on his toes all the time. People are always trying to screw him, one way or the other. I know what I'm talking about."

"You're a big help," I said.

"Now, listen, don't be disappointed if Freddie doesn't warm up to you right away. It usually takes him a little while to ... well, you know, get friendly. Hiring a private eye was H.G.'s idea. Freddie doesn't even know about it yet."

"Oh, great," I said.

"You just leave everything to me. I'll fix it up fine. I know how to handle him. I haven't been his personal manager eight years for nothing. That's a record in this business. This boy has booted the biggest of them in the ass, including MCA and Morris. Let me give you an idea how big Freddie is today. His personal income for this year alone will reach a cool four million bucks. That's a lot of loot for one little fella to earn all by himself. He makes guys like Gable and Peck look like pikers. Know what I mean?"

"Okay, I'm impressed." And I was, too.

"Well, I just wanted you to get the right slant. This is no small-time talent."

"All right, I'm sold."

Milner laughed and slapped my knee. "Makes you kind of jealous, don't it?"

I looked at him, at his gray face and pinched nostrils, and wondered if he was jealous. He had a better reason than I did.

"How about the people who work for him? How big a crew does he have?"

"Forty-six, to be exact."

I whistled through clenched teeth. "What does he do with all those people?"

"Lots of things. Besides the domestic help—you know, cooks, maids, butlers, mechanics, gardeners and people like that—he's got a personal staff. I'm his personal manager, then there's a personal business manager, a personal publicity agent, a personal secretary, a personal booking agent, a personal bodyguard and chauffeur, a personal singing coach and arranger, a personal dramatic coach, a personal make-up man, a personal writer, and there's a personal jester, a personal stooge and a personal philosopher."

"I'm not going to say a word."

"Just as well," Milner said, grinning and pinching his nostrils. "You've got a little education coming your way. You're gonna find out how the other one-half per cent lives."

We drove in silence for a while. We were going west on Sunset. At Benedict Canyon he turned north. A mile or so later he turned west again and started climbing straight up.

"He's on the top of this hill," Milner said. "Ten lush acres. The entire hilltop. On a clear day you can see the whole city lying there below you. Sometimes you can even see Catalina. And that's a good fifty, sixty miles away."

"Symbolic," I said. "The city lying at Freddie's feet. Must make him feel like a real big man."

Milner glanced at me and shrugged his narrow shoulders. "He don't need that to feel big. He is big. Look at this place. I don't know what the land cost, but the house cost him over a million. And that was a hell of a lot less than the land. Hell, the interior decorating and furnishings cost over two hundred grand. He's got offices up here, dormitories for the servants, special guest quarters for the staff. There's a dining hall with food and drinks served around the clock. He's got two tennis courts, a thirty-by-sixty swimming pool, steam rooms, a fully equipped gym, a putting green, billiard tables, and he's now planning on adding a couple of bowling alleys."

We came to a stop before a stone wall and a solid-steel gate. A small panel flipped open when Milner sounded the horn, and an eye peered out at us. Slowly, the huge gate swung open. The uniformed guard nodded politely as we drove past. Milner winked at me as we shot up the steep, winding asphalt drive.

"Man, look at that view," he said. "The best view in all of Beverly Hills."

We made a couple more sharp turns and I got my first look at the house. I've seen a lot of Hollywood-type mansions. They're all big and in my opinion ridiculous. This one was just bigger and more ridiculous. It looked like a Palm Springs hotel or one of those swanky ski lodges. You know the kind. Natural stone, glass walls and huge timbers shooting out everywhere. It was a long, sprawling structure, so low to the ground that it looked squat. That architect owed much to the landscaper. The only thing that saved his brainchild from looking like a hotel was the strategic placing of lush tropical plants. They added a softening touch that made it look almost like a house. Not quite, but almost.

"This is home," Milner said.

"I'll bet," I said.

"You'll love it here. It's gonna be a real treat for you. Good food and liquor, swimming, tennis and plenty of dolls. The place is always crawling with them." He stopped the car and bounced out. I bounced right with him.

Some character in blue slacks and red dinner jacket ran down the steps and drove away with Milner's car, goosing it all the way to the parking lot on the east side of the house by the six-car garage. I followed Milner into the house.

I wasn't disappointed. It looked exactly like a Palm Springs hotel. The living room was just as cold and artificial. Besides the floor-to-ceiling glass walls, the huge wooden beams and stone walls, there was the usual thick carpeting, the potted plants, the low-slung modern furniture and enough space in the living room alone to quarter a bivouacking company of marines. It was just as chaotic, too.

"Friends and associates," Milner said, nodding. "Mostly associates. I'll introduce you later. I think Freddie is out on the lanai."

The lanai matched the rest of the layout. It was big and it was busy. Music blasted out of at least half a dozen giant-size speakers. It was like being out at a Sunday afternoon band concert, except the music here was a damn sight louder. But what the hell, he didn't have to worry about the neighbors. A moment later I connected the voice singing over the speakers.

"Likes his voice, doesn't he?"

Milner looked at me, puzzled a moment, then grinned. "Oh, that's his latest platter. He's hearing it for the first time since cutting it two, three weeks ago."

I stayed by Milner's side as he started across the flagstone deck. I didn't particularly look around, but I did catch a few skimpy bikinis lolling around the pool. There were some fat tummies and bald heads, too. Milner stopped and held out his hand to stop me.

"Oh, Christ," he whispered. And I looked out, following the line of his gaze, and saw the golden locks and deeply tanned cheeks of Freddie Sharpe. He was sitting in a rattan chair, his long thin body folded up like a carpenter's rule, his dark eyes narrowed and smoldering as his right hand picked angrily at his outthrust lower lip. There wasn't anybody within a fifteen-foot radius of him. It was obvious that he was listening to his record, and it was equally obvious that he wasn't very damned pleased with what he was hearing.

"He's a perfectionist," Milner said in explanation. "If there's one sour note in the whole platter, he hears it like the bells of St. Mary's."

Suddenly, Sharpe shot straight up in the chair, looking frantically around the patio. "Tiny," he bellowed. "Get your ass over here."

A little guy, whom I presumed must have been Tiny, rushed by us and stopped before Freddie's chair.

"That's Tiny Tim Crosby," Milner said. "He's Freddie's singing coach and arranger."

"Well, it looks like the coach is going to hit the shower."

"Goddammit," Milner said. "We better sit down and wait a while. This is liable to take some time."

We sat down at an umbrella table. Milner crooked his finger, and the next thing I knew there was a bucket of ice, a fifth of bourbon and a carafe of water before us. I took mine on the rocks.

The music stopped, and all eyes turned to Freddie and Tiny Tim. I took a healthy swallow of bourbon and crossed my legs, leaning back in the chair to relax. Freddie was talking fast, gesticulating, his dark eyes snapping angrily. Tiny Tim just stood there with his head bowed, his small hands clenched tightly together. He looked like a little kid about to be spanked. He kept nodding and shifting his feet. At first Freddie's voice was too low for me to get the message, but the more he talked the louder it became, until finally everybody in Beverly Hills could hear him, ten acres notwithstanding.

"You stupid sonofabitch," he said, sitting up straight in the chair and pointing a stiff finger at Tiny Tim's head. It looked as menacing as the barrel of a .45. "I told you I didn't like that crummy arrangement. Well, did you hear it just now? Did you, goddammit?"

Tiny Tim's mouth opened and closed, but nothing came out. His face had a sickly pallor. I felt sorry for the little fellow, being bawled out like that in front of everybody and no way of defending himself. My opinion of that sweet, generous Freddie was being confirmed the first two minutes on the job.

"What was the payola on that one, you Judas?" He waited for an answer, and when it didn't come he threw himself back in his chair, waving his arms in dismissal. "Ah, for Christ's sake. Get out of my sight. You make me sick, you creepy little runt. Go on, crawl back in your hole, you lousy little thief."

Tiny Tim spun around and ran into the house. I caught a glimpse of his face as he dashed by me, and it wasn't pretty to see. But I couldn't very much blame him for thinking those ugly thoughts.

"He's a sweet boy, all right," I said, pouring myself another slug of bourbon. "Beloved by one and all, I'm sure."

Milner cleared his throat and gave me a sidelong glance. "What the hell," he said. "He's got to be tough with these babies. He's on top of the heap now, but how long do you think he'd last if he wasn't tough? He knows what he's doing. Nobody's gonna knock this kid off. He knows how to handle himself. You can take my word for that."

"I don't know," I said. "Maybe, they'll knock him off for good. With a gun."

"Jesus! don't talk like that," Milner said, his gray face even grayer, if possible.

"Gus!"

Milner jumped like someone had struck him with a bayonet. "Yeah, sweetheart, I'm coming," he called, that painted smile back on his kisser. "Come on," he whispered to me. "I'll introduce you."

"I love your timing," I said, getting up.

The lower lip was stuck out again and the dark eyes were still smoldering, but now in my direction.

"I want *Love Me Now* taken out of the album. Make arrangements for a recording session tonight."

"Freddie, sweetheart, it's too late. I was talking to Frank just this morning. It's already being pressed. Hundreds have gone out to the deejays."

Freddie slammed his fist against the arm of the chair. "Who told him to press? I retain the final right of approval. Or don't I any more? Maybe you do. Is that it?"

"I didn't tell Frank anything. I guess he thought you were satisfied with it."

"What a goddam organization. Everybody is out to ruin me. Who the hell do you work for? Who? Go on, tell me. I'd like to know."

"But sweetheart ..."

"You don't work for me. That's for sure. Now, I want you to make up your mind. Right now. Who do you work for?"

"You, baby. We all love you. You know that. This is just a little mistake. Frank jumped the gun. It's not so bad. Frankly, I like it. It's got a nice beat to it."

"Oh, you like it. What the hell do you know about a beat? For Christ's sake."

His eyes kept shifting toward me during the tirade. Now he pointed that stiff finger at my head. "Who's he?"

"I'm a music critic," I said. "And I agree with you. It stinks."

Milner coughed nervously and looked at me like I had just lost my mind. "He's only kidding, baby. He—"

"Shut up," Freddie said. "So you think it stinks, eh?"

"Yeah. That's what I said."

There was a softening in the dark eyes. He leaned back and brought up his long spindly legs into the chair, hugging them to his chest.

"What do you know about it?"

"Presley should sing that number. It's strictly rock-and-roll. It doesn't swing."

Suddenly he was smiling, and, dammit, H.G. was right. It was electric. His whole face lit up, and I found myself smiling back. I couldn't help it. It was that infectious. Those porcelain caps just about blinded me.

"What's your name?"

"Slader."

"Put it here, Slader," he said, offering me his hand. His hand-shake was warm and firm. For the first time, Milner was smiling for real.

"Sit down and have a drink," Freddie said.

"Sweetheart," Milner said, his face anxious again. "Can we have a little talk, just the three of us, in private?"

Freddie looked at me, then back at Milner. "Slader," he mused, pulling on his ear lobe. "I've heard that name before."

"Come on, baby, this is private," Milner said, quickly looking around the lanai to see if anyone was listening. He lowered his voice to a whisper. "It's about that stuff H. G. is holding."

Freddie slapped his thigh. "You're a shamus," he said, jumping out of the chair. "Come on, I want to talk to you."

Milner and I followed him into the house. People really moved out of his way. Milner caught up to him in the living room, but I stayed a few steps behind. He had an interesting walk, the kind some people get when they become too important. It was a mixture of humility and calculated arrogance. Somehow it added to his stature. Freddie was about six-one or two, and bone-thin. Comedians had been poking fun at his bean-pole physique for years. But on him that bag of bones looked good.

He ducked into a room and I went in after him. There was a blonde lying on a red leather couch, reading a movie maga-zine. She turned her head slightly to look at us, then returned her attention to the latest Hollywood gossip.

"Sit down," Freddie said, moving in behind a modern walnut desk. "This is Marsha," he added nodding toward the blonde. She continued to read. "She's my personal secretary."

"That's nice."

Freddie clapped his hands. "Hear that, baby? You've got an admirer."

"That's nice," she said, still reading.

"How about the nice secretary?" I said. "Is she in on this?"

Freddie waved his hands impatiently. "She's in. Go ahead, spill it."

"Well, sweetheart," Milner began, nervous again, his nose twitching. "H.G. sent him over to be your bodyguard. He's real worried about those threats. You know, he loves you like a son and he'll do everything in his power to protect you."

"Cut the horsecrap," Freddie said. "I know what he's protecting."

"Now, wait a minute, sweetheart. H.G. is sincere."

"I don't need protection. Sorry, Slader."

"No, no," Milner protested. "I think H.G. is right this time. You do need protection. This crackpot might really try to knock you off or something. Slader, here, can stop him. That's his business. He's the best in the business. H.G. really screened the field. You know H.G. Always nothing but the best."

"I'm getting goddam sick of H.G.," Freddie said. "You tell him for me to keep his goddam blue beak out of my business."

"What's your objection?" I said.

"Publicity. Some wise reporter gets wind of this and I'll be splashed over every front page in the country. I don't want that kind of public relations. It's a killer. I know big careers that were snapped off just like that." He winked and snapped his fingers.

"But who's to know?" Milner insisted. "Only the four of us and H.G. know about it. How are they going to find out?"

"How the hell do I know? All I know is those bastards always find out."

"Look," I said. "What's more important? Your public relations or your life? Make a choice."

Marsha slowly sat up and stretched. I could almost hear the purring. "Freddie," she said, lazily as hell. "You better keep the nice admirer. I have a stinking suspicion the press already knows about it."

"You what!" he screamed, glaring fiercely at all three of us as though we were conspirators. I could see Milner shrinking in his cashmere jacket. Freddie's hot glare was sapping all the juice out of him.

"Now, Freddie," Marsha said, crossing her long legs. "Screaming won't do any good. I'm merely expressing an opinion. Or rather my feminine intuition."

"Cut it," he said. "That feminine intuition don't cut no ice with me. Let's have it."

"I swear it. I don't know a damn thing."

He looked at her a long time. Those smoldering black eyes never blinked once. She was all right for a while, but then the cool pose started to melt. And that was the end of it. Slowly, she dropped her gaze to her hands and stood up jerkily.

"I need a drink," she said, trying to recapture some of the frost of a moment ago, but by now it was just a puddle of tepid water. Even so she struck a responsive cord in my spine as she long-legged it across the room, the light summer skirt dinging to her hips like a surgical glove. She stopped before a leather-covered bar and quickly fixed herself a drink.

"Anybody else want a drink?" she asked, lifting up her glass in mocked gaiety.

"Yeah," I said. "I'll have one." I got up and went over to the bar. From the corner of my eye, I saw Milner jump up and scurry over to Freddie's desk.

"Do you fix it or do I?"

"I'm busy," she said, and damn near downed the whole drink in one gulp.

"Take it easy," I said. "He's only a singer."

"That's all you know," she said, plunking her empty glass on the bar. "Make yourself useful, shamus."

At the desk, Milner was whispering frantically into Freddie's ear and Freddie was shaking his head just as frantically in the negative.

I fixed myself a solid jolt of bourbon and handed her a refill, holding on to the glass a moment before releasing it. She looked directly into my eyes and I smiled, trying my damnedest to relax her. She had a nice face and beautiful deep-amber-colored eyes. Slowly, the corners of her mouth turned up, and for a fleeting second a smile danced in those amber pools.

"That's all I wanted," I said, going back to my chair.

Milner was still whispering, but Freddie had stopped objecting. He just stared at me with those black eyes, now without expression.

"Okay, okay," he said, pushing Milner away from him.

Milner straightened up but remained by Freddie's chair. "Vince," he said. "In view of the situation, we want you to stay. You know, of course, Freddie already has a bodyguard. What we're gonna do is give the Killer a vacation. That way it will look like you just came in as a replacement. No reason for anybody to get suspicious."

"Sounds okay to me," I said. "Although there are a few things I want to get straightened out right from the beginning."

"Sure, Vince," Milner said. "Lay it on the line."

"I'm your bodyguard twenty-four hours a day. You don't do anything or go anywhere without me. From now on any shadow you cast is going to have a double image."

"Now, wait a minute," Freddie said. "Don't get carried away."

"Listen, Freddie, you're interested in your public relations. Well, so am I interested in my public relations. That's all I have to sell in my business. I'm here to prevent a murder, not to solve one. And that's the way it's going to be. Otherwise, you better call H.G. and tell him to do some more screening."

Freddie didn't say anything for a while, but he was doing plenty of thinking. "You take those screwy notes pretty seriously, don't you?"

"Why not? You wouldn't be the first guy to get knocked off by some jerk with a grudge. You might be the biggest man in this town, but your hide is just as penetrable as the smallest one. All it takes is one tiny slug of lead and you can forget all about that publicity." I was laying it on pretty thick, but what the hell—a grand a week and high-class nookie don't grow on a bush. And, besides, the guy could actually be in danger. At least, that's the way I had to look at it. Otherwise, you usually find out when it's too late.

"Okay, Slader, you're in. But don't carry this housemother bit too far. There are times when I need privacy, if you know what I mean."

"I know. But you won't mind if I listen, as long as I don't look?"

3

FREDDIE AND Milner left, and Marsha was entrusted with my care. She waited until we were alone to refill her glass.

"One more," she said. "And I'll take you out to the Zoo."

She was breathing more easily now, and a slight smile curved her lips. She was a very attractive dame.

"You better have another one yourself," she said. "It's good for what ails you."

"I'm not ailing."

She grinned. "You will be."

"Pretty grim, eh?"

"The grimmest. I'm going to introduce you to the greatest live animal act in captivity."

"You included?"

"Me included."

She tilted up the glass and drained it in one gulp. Her hand shook a little when she reached for the bottle. She was taking it straight now.

"Always drihk this much?"

"What's that supposed to mean?"

The remark had insulted her. In my book, that's a bad sign. If you can't talk about your drinking, you're usually in trouble.

I held up my hands in surrender. "Just a stupid observation. My apologies."

"Christ," she said, getting angrier. "If there's anything I hate it's a goddam mealy-mouthed hypocrite."

Everybody was running true to form in this joint. It might seem like a zoo to her, but to me it looked more like a psychopathic ward.

"Drink it down," I said. "And let's get to work."

"There's no rush. They're not going anywhere." She took a deep breath, and it put a hell of a strain on the buttons of that silk blouse. She was well equipped for her job. But then there are very few flat-chested dames around this neck of the woods.

"Who's first on the list?"

She considered that for a moment, twisting her mouth. "Junior."

"Who's Junior?"

"Marty Lewis. Publicity."

"He doesn't sound like your favorite."

"He's a weasel. Know what that is?"

"I have a fairly good idea. How long has he been around?"

"Six months. But that's longer than the other four weasels before him. Right now, he's hanging on by his toenails, and doing plenty of scratching in a lot of sensitive places."

Marty Lewis was on the telephone when we arrived in his private cubbyhole. He winked at Marsha and waved to me like we were old buddies.

"That's right, Sarah, dear," he was saying. "Freddie really fractured the table. You bet. Thought you might like that little *bon mot* for your column. Always thinking of you, dear. What's that? Oh, sure, everything's going along swell. That's right. Leaving Monday for location. Freddie is superb in the role. Sure to cop an Oscar. You bet, sweetheart. Just as soon as he gets back from Kansas. We'll all get together for a nice little interview. Freddie loves you, dear. Why, hell, just this morning he said to me, 'Call Sarah and tell her I love her more than ever.' He has nothing but the deepest affection for you. I mean it, dear. That's what the man said. Okay. Will see you in three weeks. By-by."

He dropped the receiver and rolled his eyes. "The bitch," he said. "She'd sell her mother into white slavery for an ounce of dirt."

"Wouldn't we all, though," Marsha said, slumping into a chair. "This is Vince Slader. Freddie's new bodyguard."

"Oh," he said.

"The Killer is going on vacation."

"You mean pasture, don't you?"

"No. I mean vacation."

"Okay, dear, I get you. Slader? I know that name. You're a private dick. I've read about you. Getting up in the world."

"Private investigator," I said. "And right now I'm slumming."

"Touché," he said.

Marsha looked at me and raised her eyebrows. "This is not for release," she said.

"It's not? Listen, this guy's got a rep in Hollywood. Be a good publicity angle. I could dig up a couple of his sensational cases and tie the whole package up real neat."

"Down, boy. Or Freddie will spank."

"I'll talk to Freddie myself. I'll bet he goes for it."

"You do that," she said. "And good luck." She stood up and motioned for me to follow.

"Listen, Slader," he said, when I had reached the door. "Nice to have you aboard."

I nodded and got the hell out, bumping into Marsha outside the door. She was soft in all the right places. My pulse did a quick skip and jump. "Sorry," I said. "I didn't mean to get personal."

She didn't move away. "Well, that's a switch around here."

"Who's next?" I said, shoving my hands in my pockets.

"We'll take potluck. Let's case the living room."

We walked into that glacial lobby again and she stopped, gripping my arm to hold me back.

"Over there," she said, pointing. "In the corner. See the big guy with the pipe and the good-looking Negro sitting next to him? That's Carlton Stone and Matthew Fowler, old bear and wise owl."

"Let me guess," I said. "Stone is the personal writer."

"Give that man a plugged sheckle. How did you guess?"

"The good old briar. Dead giveaway. Looks like he's waiting to have his picture taken for the back of a book-of-the-month jacket. What's Fowler?"

"He's the personal philosopher. Ph.D. from U.C.L.A. A walking encyclopedia and a good guy. Spends his time briefing Freddie on world affairs. His daddy broke his black back putting him through college so he could discuss international politics with a goddam singer."

"There are worse jobs," I said, gazing at the two men. Stone was probably in his late thirties. He looked well fed and adjusted to his environment. He had thick brown curly hair and a round face that was a little too red to be healthy. Fowler, very thin and ascetic-looking, looked more Indian than Negro.

"Come on. I'll introduce you."

"Wait. Point out a few more of these characters first. I'll get around to talking to them later."

"Look over there. See the little fat guy in the baggy pants? That's Chauncey, the personal clown. Does pratfalls by the hour to amuse Freddie. Was the biggest clown of his day. But now all he's good for is a personal pratfall when Freddie is depressed. Makes you sick, don't it?"

I remembered Chauncey. He had been world-famous at one time. He had made a million kids laugh and a million parents cry. He had been that kind of a performer. He had dispensed pathos and humor with the same deft touch that spelled greatness.

"I saw him," I said. "When I was just a kid. He made me laugh."

"Yeah," she said. "Well, he makes me cry."

"Who else?"

"See that black vulture over there? The one with the Auntie Mame cigarette holder? That's Phemie White, the personal dramatic coach. She makes me want to puke."

"What's the matter with her?"

"She's made more passes at me than all the creeps that ever crawled into this dump. Now she's working on Adela Adams, a sixteen-year-old kid from Nebraska."

"Where is she?"

"She's not here. She's in *Run for Home*. If Phemie doesn't get into bed with her before that picture is in the can, I'll swallow that holder."

"It's quite a crew," I said. She didn't have to tell me about Phemie White. It couldn't have been plainer if it had been stamped on her forehead in forty-eight-point type. She didn't only brandish a cigarette holder like Mame, she dressed like her, too. She looked like some Lesbian suddenly resurrected from the roaring twenties.

"The guy she's talking to is Loren Mayberry, the personal make-up—pardon the expression—man. He's as queer as she is, but not quite so blunt about it. At least, he doesn't go around pinching the boys. Though I think he'd like to, especially some of the cuties who come around here all the time."

"He's in the right business."

"You can say that twice. That's all I can see right now. Ray Martin, the business manager, and Al Goldstein, the booking agent, are both out of town. Oh, there's Rocco Scarpianno, more affectionately known as the Rock. He's Freddie's first cousin and personal stooge."

"Scarpianno?" I said. "That's a familiar name."

"Why not? It's Freddie's real name. Frederico Scarpianno." She gave the pronunciation a thick Italian accent. "Don't tell him I told you. He'd kill me."

"Nothing wrong with Scarpianno," I said. "It's a good Italian name. What has he got to be ashamed of?"

"Oh, hell, we both don't have the time to go into *that* dreary subject."

"Leave anybody out?"

"Oh, let's see. Yeah, there's Abe Schwartz, the personal accountant. But you never see him. He's always hiding somewhere in a ledger. He's the one guy Freddie can't argue with. He's got it all there in black and white."

"How about red?"

"What's that? Abe doesn't even own a bottle of red ink. This is strictly a paying proposition. Everybody is getting rich and going to an analyst. Great fun. You'll love it here."

"I might if you're nice to me."

She gave me a cold sidelong glance. "You catch on fast," she said. "You'll make out just fine in this snakepit."

"What's the matter? You got something against sex? It existed a long time before Hollywood. Actually, you know, it's for everybody, rich or poor, movie star or private eye. It's all the same. Nobody has a priority on it. That's what I like about a democracy."

"Excuse me," she said. "I have a date with a bottle. There are a couple of sexpots by the pool. Try your luck out there."

"Thanks for the suggestion," I said. "I'll see what I can dig up."

After she left, I wandered around the house for half an hour or so without anyone ever so much as glancing at me. Finally I sat by the pool and had a couple of bourbons. The sexpots in the bikinis were still there, lying on their backs, giving that old red-eyed sun a break. I didn't venture any propositions. They looked like they already belonged in somebody's stable, somebody with a lot bigger bundle than I had. Gus Milner came dashing by, and I stopped him.

"I think I better go home and pack a bag. Then I'd like to sit down with Freddie and work out the details."

"Sure, sure, Vince. Go ahead. Everything's under control here."

4

THE TRIP down to my apartment gave me a moment for some aimless thoughts, which was about all I could muster at this stage of the game. Anonymous threats to a public figure are fairly common. They are usually written by lonely, twisted but harmless people seeking a cheap thrill. The fact that there was no demand for money took the sting out of the notes. The only other consideration, of course, was Freddie himself and the enemies he had made on those climbs up to the top. But that was a bigger bite than I wanted to chew on at the time.

My apartment is on the Sunset Strip, which is in the county of Los Angeles and outside of city jurisdiction. I like it better this way. For one thing, it is easier for a private investigator to obtain a gun permit from the sheriff's office. The L.A. cops frown on the practice.

The apartment is not only my home, but also my place of business. It is three rooms on the second floor of a pink stucco building typical of the Strip. I have a small balcony in the back with a nice view of the city—not as great as Freddie's, but great enough for me. I like to sit out there in the evening with a cool drink and watch the lights of the city twinkle in the smog. I'm the only guy I know who doesn't mind the smog. Los Angeles doesn't have a priority on it. I've never seen a big city without it, here or abroad. The only difference is that they talk about it more here than anywhere else. That's because this was a cow town fifty years ago and nobody had a chance to get used to the big city atmosphere. One day they were breathing the sweet smell of horse manure and the next morning they were coughing in the industrial fumes.

When I got to the apartment, I decided to shower and shave. Then I flopped on the sofa in the living room, called my answering service and told Polly where I'd be until further notice. The name Freddie Sharpe made her voice leap across the line.

"How old are you, Polly?" I asked. She had only been a dull voice up to now.

"Thirty-two. Why?"

"Just making sure you're not a bobby soxer."

"I used to be one. Gosh, I was just crazy about Freddie when I was sixteen and seventeen."

"Not now, though, eh?"

"Well, it's different now. But I still like him a lot."

"Why is that?"

"Because he's—Oh, go on, you're pulling my leg."

"No, I'm serious. I'd like to know."

"Gee, I don't know. He's got a nice voice." She hesitated a moment. "And he's still real cute."

"Thanks, Polly. Be a good girl while I'm gone."

"What else?" she said. "I'm too old to be bad."

I hung up and started to pack. Then I went into the kitchen and fed the garbage disposer some fresh meat and vegetables. I looked at the temperature dial on the refrigerator and hopefully turned it to "vacation." I mixed myself an honest drink and went back into the living room. I selected a Freddie Sharpe album and sat on the sofa with my long legs stretched out across the coffee table, gently pulling at the drink. The guy did have a nice voice. And he knew how to use it. Very tricky phrasing, clear, sharp delivery and a tonal quality all of his own. But no matter how you sliced it, it didn't add up to four million a year. Even in Hollywood, it was a ridiculous sum. That would pay the President's salary for the next thirty-five, forty years. And, for my money, the President was cuter. But

OVID DEMARIS

then, Polly was not likely to buy any of his records. And the
newsreels were free.

After a couple of numbers, I switched it off and left the precious solitude of my apartment for that psycho ward on a hilltop
in Beverly Hills, and a grand per week. Money can make a hell of
a deafening sound.

The sun was timidly hiding behind Freddie's private hilltop
when I drove into the parking lot. A cool ocean breeze had come up,
and palm fronds rustled gently above my head. Below me the city
was getting its second wind, bolstering itself for another assault of
gaiety and grief. I felt strange, almost omnipotent, standing there,
watching the street lights flash on in long neat rows. It's a big city,
nearly five hundred square miles, and I had examined its most
intimate parts. Now, from up here, it seemed like it belonged to
me. Like I could make it disappear with a wave of my hand. Lust,
power, greed, hope, despair, charity, love—all sterile, meaningless
words for a God on a hilltop. I shook my head and started walking
toward the house. Goddam, I thought. Some shamus.

Except for a couple of Filipino houseboys in their red and
blue outfits, the living room was deserted. The boys quickly spotted me and hurried over, grinning and bowing as they wrenched
the bags from my hands. They didn't know who I was, but they
sure as hell knew where I belonged.

The bedroom wasn't exactly on the plush side, but it was adequate, with a large, comfortable-looking bed, a dresser, a small
writing desk and a couple of overstuffed chairs. The pictures on
the walls were expensive reproductions of abstract art. The kind
of stuff that's supposed to tickle your psyche without letting it
know why.

While they unpacked my bags, I walked around the room,
trying the various doors. Two for the wardrobe, one for the
adjoining bathroom, one locked.

"Where does this door lead to?" I asked, rattling the
doorknob.

"That's Mr. Sharpe's bedroom, sir."

"Is he in, do you know?"

"No, sir. Mr. Sharpe has left for the evening."

The news didn't exactly come as a shock to me. "How about Mr. Milner?"

"He's gone, too, sir."

"Did they leave any message for me?"

He shrugged his shoulders in typical oriental fashion. "Don't know. Maybe Miss Miles knows."

"Who's Miss Miles?"

They both looked at me like I had lost my mind.

"Never mind," I said. "I know. She's Mr. Sharpe's personal secretary."

My sudden recovery pleased them both immensely.

"Where's the dining room?"

"I'll show you, sir. Come with me."

I damn near had to run to keep up with him. Those rugged little bowlegs rolled up that hallway like a runaway wheel.

"Right here," he said, bowing again.

"Thanks," I said, and pushed through the swinging door.

This time I was surprised. I had to stop and wait for my eyes to adjust to the dim light. The room was small, with a low ceiling, and red leather-covered booths and chairs. I had expected a cafeteria with glaring lights and stainless steel fixtures. Instead I found a Sunset Strip bistro.

I stopped at the first empty table in my path and was immediately handed a tabloid-size menu by another Filipino. This one was dad in spotless white linen. The menu had three entrees—prime rib, turkey and roast pork. I ordered prime rib and a Caesar salad.

"Wine, sir?" he said, flipping the menu over to give me a look at the wine list. I selected Cabernet Sauvignon.

I took my time eating. I was in no hurry. With Freddie and Milner gone, all I could do was sit and twiddle my thumbs. At the moment I felt like a doctor who diagnoses an illness only to be ignored by the patient. The main difference was that I didn't give a particular damn. Freddie was at least thirty-seven years old, which made him old enough to be responsible for himself. If he didn't take the threat seriously, then why should I tear my hair out? Even so, I felt a little peeved that my warning had fallen on deaf ears. I suppose the big thing here was that I didn't truly feel he was in danger.

"Mr. Slader?"

I looked up and saw the smiling, chubby face of Carlton Stone. He was offering me his hand. I shook it without getting up.

"Carlton Stone," he said, looking at the empty chair.

"Sit down," I said. "And tell me your problem."

"Problem? What's that?"

"No problem? Then what the hell are you doing here?"

"Man," he grinned. "I'm lying here, comfortable as hell, in my nice silken casket."

"Sounds cozy. Any extra room in there?"

"Room? Man there's ten acres of it. Enough room to bury every goddam artist in Hollywood."

"And you don't have a problem?"

"No, man, I make it like euphoria. Wow!"

I looked at him, not knowing whether he was on or for real. "Whatsa matter, man, you dig that Kerouac bit?"

He laughed, taking out his pipe and blowing noisily through the stem.

"Not really," he said. "I usually try to please Bergen Evans."

"Well, if you've got to please somebody, I suppose he's about as good as any of them."

"Ah, a nonconformist has joined our ranks. What exactly is your position here?"

"Bodyguard."

"Permanent or transient?"

"A little of both."

"Evasive, too."

"Not yet."

"I hear the Killer is not too happy about his unexpected furlough."

"Well, that's too bad. I'm sorry to hear it."

"The Killer is a very jealous man. Might not take too kindly to a stranger kicking him out of the nuptial bed."

"Thanks for the tip, I think." I pushed my chair back and stood up. "See you around."

"Keep a stiff eye out for Freddie," he said. "We all love him dearly."

After that I wandered about the place. With Freddie gone things had really petered out. I saw Fowler in the living room. He was talking to Chauncey, who was listening with his mouth wide open, enraptured by the great words of wisdom from the personal philosopher. A couple of characters were playing chess, and some redhead was stretched out seductively across a sofa, her black dress pulled up to disclose a generous slice of pure white thighs. I kept walking.

Finally I decided to get a bottle and retire to my adequate room. The enclosing walls would be a relief and comfort after the wide-open spaces I'd been treading. I crooked my finger at a houseboy on my way and ordered ice and a bottle of bourbon. The best. I got it five minutes later. And it was the best. I took off my jacket and tie, rolled up my shirt cuffs and kicked off my shoes. I loosened my belt and slipped off the belt holster with the .38 special tucked inside. Then I propped up the pillows on the bed and stretched out. There was a small transistor radio on the night stand, and I tuned in a music station. Freddie sang to me while I guzzled his bonded bourbon.

5

I T DIDN'T take long. Less than an hour and she was scratch-at my bedroom door. I stayed down on the bed, holding the cold drink against my cheek.

"Come in," I called, "whoever the hell you are." I knew who it was, all right; but at the moment it wouldn't have been polite to admit it.

Her entrance was charming—blonde hair disheveled, lipstick on crooked, mascara smeared at the inside corners. She leaned against the door and slowly, carefully ran her tongue across her upper lip.

"Hi," she said. "Lonely?"

"Very. First night away from home and all that sad jazz."

"I thought so," she said, carefully navigating across the room, bottle in one hand, cigarette in the other. "Let's have a drink and happy jazz each other up real good." She placed the bottle on the night stand next to mine. Mine was in a lot healthier condition.

"What's this? Drinking gin now?"

"Passion juice, lover," she said. "Very good for little zombies."

"Back to that again? Still in the land of the walking dead?"

"Never left and never will. Here," she said, sitting on the edge of the bed. "Unzip me like a good little lecher. I feel hot all over."

"It is a warm night," I said, doing as the lady ordered. "That's an interesting tan. Belong to a nudist camp?"

She giggled. "Got a secret nest." She stood up and let the dress fall to the floor. And that was it. The only thing left was her well-roasted epidermis.

"How's your tan? Peel the shirt, friend, show the lady."

"I don't need a tan. I'm naturally dark-skinned."

"Show me."

"Sure, Marsha, baby." I sat up and slipped out of my shirt.

"Oooh," she cooed, her red lips puckering. "You've got muscles. Big ones. Can I touch them?"

"Why not, as long as it's reciprocal."

"That's a big word for a shamus," she said, pressing both her hands against my chest and slowly working down.

"Come closer," I said. "And I'll talk only in four-letter words."

"Will you?" she whispered, her breath catching in her throat. Suddenly she dropped against me, her teeth going after my ear. I ran my hands down her soft back to her rounded buttocks, and it was not hot at all. In fact, it was as smooth and cool as a piece of ice sculpture.

"I'm gonna like this," she said, while I squeezed her in all the right places. "After all the pansies digging this dump, it's good to have a man again."

"Don't con me," I said. "A dame with your looks has no trouble getting a man. Not if she really wants one."

"What do you know," she said. "You're just a dumb shamus. Dumb but oooh are you virile."

"That's right," I said. "I never argue with a lady I'm about to lay. It spoils the rapport."

"There you go again, destroying the image. Remember, four-letter words?"

"How can I forget?" I said, whispering a few choice ones in her delicate ear. The words were the catalyst. She really started working in earnest after that.

But it didn't last long. The next thing I knew, the bedroom door slammed against the wall and the whole room shook with palsy. I jumped up in the bed, staring at the biggest bastard I'd ever seen tearing through any door of mine.

"My God," Marsha cried, crawling away from me in terror.

"What the hell is that?" I asked.

"It's the Killer, and he's crazy drunk."

"Slader!" he bellowed, kicking the door shut with a foot as large as an elephant. "Get out of that bed!"

I don't know how many times I had heard that name in the last few hours, but not once had I made the connection with Killer Storm. Now I did. He had been a contender for the heavyweight championship of the world at least half a dozen times in the late thirties and early forties. He had never made it, but it wasn't because he was too small. He was gargantuan, almost as big as Camera. From my sitting position on the bed, he looked even bigger than he had at ringside. I'm six-three, but this pug had a good four inches on me, plus at least seventy-five pounds. This was something I hadn't counted on. I looked up into that drunken, ravaged face and tried to smile the butterflies away. But those dull beady eyes looked like they were imbedded in solid concrete. The butterflies flapped and scurried like an army of bats balling out of a cave at sundown.

"Take it easy, Killer," I said, as calmly as I could under the circumstances.

"Get up," he snarled, weaving toward me.

His clenched fists looked like steel mallets. The law states that a fighter's fists are deadly weapons. I never agreed more sadly with a statute.

"What's the beef, friend? I don't even know you."

"You dirty sonofabitch," he growled, grabbing my ankle and twisting it. "I'll show you who's Freddie's bodyguard."

Grabbing my ankle was his first mistake. His second was thinking he was still in Madison Square Garden, fighting under the rules of the New York Boxing Commission.

He had a firm hold of my left ankle and was peering drunkenly down at me. I smiled sweetly and lashed out with my right foot, pounding my leather heel into his mid-section with everything I had. Christ, it was like kicking a stone wall. It was a good thing I still had my shoes on. Otherwise I would have pulverized my foot.

He grunted hoarsely and let go of the ankle, staggering back toward the door. I didn't wait for an invitation to get up. He saw me coming and his fantastic shoulders bunched up like a rhino's about to charge, his small bullet head disappearing behind the bulging muscles.

Good Christ, I thought. This guy's been in the same ring with Louis. The only ring I'd been in had solid walls on two sides and trash cans at each end. You never got time to learn a boxing style. All you did was try to hit faster and harder than the other guy. And you did it any goddam way you could—with a fist, a gun butt, a club or a foot. It wasn't how you played the game that counted, it was how healthy you were when you staggered out.

His feet shifted quickly in that typical boxing shuffle, knees bending, shoulders rolling, left hand tapping the air in front of my nose, right hand cocked and loaded with sudden and violent death.

I really felt like talking then. I probably would have said anything to get spirited out of that room in one piece. Anything, and yet nothing came out. I couldn't utter a word. I guess if you're a little guy you can cry your way out. But when you're my size there's no other way out but the hard way.

I could hear Marsha's heavy breathing behind me on the bed, but I didn't have time to worry about her trauma. I was having one of my own.

I waited for him, hoping to get a couple of solid belts in before he laid me out. Then he made his move. One moment he was doing his cute little dance, and the next second he was just a blur. Lights burst in my head and a hurricane exploded in my stomach. I felt myself propelled into violent motion—backward motion, sending me reeling against the bed, my body spinning sideways so that I landed face down on the mattress. I hadn't even landed a love pat.

"Get up," he ordered, dancing away, waiting for me to return to battle after the count of nine.

I took my time getting up, exaggerating the grogginess, and staggered toward him, my fists hanging limply at my sides. He was grinning now, his thick gladiator lips wet with small bubbles of saliva, his round hard eyes glinting under the heavy tissue-scarred brows. I kept staggering until I was so close to him I could smell his foul breath.

He was enjoying himself, playing a cat-and-mouse game, savoring the moment when he would deliver the kill. He waited too long. I hit him with the hardest combination in my sordid repertoire. The back of my left fist, followed by a solid right cross. It cracked against the tip of his granite jaw like a single explosion. I felt bone splinter. The pain shot up my left arm all the way to my brain, and I nearly passed out.

His knees buckled slightly, but only slightly, as he shuffled back, his small eyes blinking with the pain. I rushed in and slammed the edge of my fist into his exposed throat. Spittle burst from his slack mouth and his eyes swelled grotesquely. I was back in the alley. My knee shot up into the soft cartilage of his groin. He doubled over so fast his nose hit my thigh. I pounded him in the neck with half a dozen rabbit punches, then my knee came up again and slammed into his face. His head flew back, his huge arms flailing the air for balance. I looked at his jutting chin and changed my mind. Once was enough. I lashed out with my foot and drop-kicked him where he lived. He hit the wall like an earthquake and slowly sank to the floor, his head coming to rest on his knees.

I turned and staggered to the bed, gasping for breath. I looked up into the bright luminous eyes of Marsha and backed away, going for the bottle on the night stand. I heard her bare feet on the floor behind me, then her arms circled my waist.

"Vince," she whispered hoarsely. "Love me. Love me now. Quick."

I raised the bottle and let the warm liquid gurgle down my throat. "I've had all the exercise I want for one night," I said. I knew what she was getting at. That look in her eyes had told me all I needed to know. I try to stay clear of dames with a sadistic bent. It leads to nasty complications.

She was pressing her body against mine, and I tried to move away without offending her, but it was useless.

"Let go," I said. "I'm not in the mood."

She held on for dear life. "Please, Vince. Take me."

"Goddammit," I said, grabbing her wrist and twisting it sharply. "I said let go. And while you're at it, get lost."

She stared at me, wide-eyed, then spun around and ran from the room, naked as the day she was born. I looked down at the unconscious Killer and sighed. Now that it was all over, I could feel a little pity. He had never been great but he had been up there, a lot higher than most boxers ever reached. Twenty years ago the Killer would have killed me on the spot without a change of wind. I sat on the bed and took another pull from the bottle. My left hand had begun to swell, and I could feel the knuckles getting stiff. That backhand was not as good as I had thought. And it would be a lot worse for a long time to come.

I slipped back into my shirt and opened the night stand drawer, fishing out the .38 special and belt holster. I wanted it on me before he came to. No need to press my luck too far. Once around the hard way with the Killer was once too many for my sporting blood. After I had the old equalizer tucked securely at my side, I went into the bathroom and looked around for a container. The biggest thing I could find was a water glass. I filled it, went out to the Killer and splashed it in his face. He didn't flick a muscle. What I needed was a fire hose.

I was on my way for a refill when Gus Milner burst into the room, his usually gray face a sickly green. He was out of breath, and his hands shook badly when he raised them toward me.

"Vince," he gasped, struggling to control his breathing. "It's Freddie. He was in an accident on his way to Palm Springs."

I took him by the arm and sat him on the bed, grabbing for the bottle. "Here, take a good pull and calm down."

"He's hurt and in the hospital. We've got to go to him right away."

"Sure, Gus. But take it easy for a second. Come on, drink it down."

The liquor spilled down his chin and tears flooded his eyes. I didn't know whether he was crying for Freddie or the liquor was too raw for his throat.

"What happened?" he said, startled by the limp form of the Killer slumped against the wall.

"Never mind him. How badly is Freddie hurt?"

"I don't know. So help me Christ, Vince, those bastards wouldn't tell me a goddam thing on the phone."

"Okay," I said. "If you're feeling better we'll go."

He pointed a shaky finger at the Killer. "I wanted him to drive."

"I'll drive."

"I can get the Rock. It's a long drive, and the Rock likes it. I think he ought to come anyway. Freddie might need him."

"Fine," I said, going to the closet for my jacket. I gave the Killer one last, sad look and followed Milner out into the hall.

Rocco Scarpianno, the Rock, had been Freddie's number-one personal stooge for over ten years. I didn't know how much he liked being a stooge, but it was obvious that he liked to drive. He handled Milner's Cadillac like he was part of its mechanism.

I sat in the back with Gus and did some thinking. It was going to be a long drive and I didn't much feel like small talk. This had been one hell of a day, and the way it looked it wasn't over yet.

I gazed out the window and saw that we were speeding along Olympic Boulevard in West Los Angeles. Ahead, and to my left, I could make out the dark shadowy outlines of the huge sound stages at Goldman Studios. I glanced at my watch. It was two minutes past midnight. It was hard to believe that only ten hours earlier I had entered those most hallowed grounds in search, not of religion, but of easy loot.

6

N OT TOO many years ago Palm Springs was a small desert outpost. Today it is a lush oasis existing solely for the titillation and scampering of bored movie stars. It has the kind of tinseled appeal that strikes at the very nerve center of the Hollywood glamour. The door knobs are just as big as in Beverly Hills, the swimming pools as cutely designed, the landscaping as garishly bourgeois, the week-end guests as hopelessly neurotic. Nothing in Palm Springs is for real. The place makes about as much sense as a Cinemascope musical.

It was nearly two o'clock when we drove into the parking lot at the hospital. Freddie was waiting for us in the Chief-of-Staff's private office. His thin face was pale beneath the thick layers of tan, and his left eye was swollen shut. There was a long strip of tape running along the edge of his chin. He looked old and shrunken and frightened.

"Baby, baby," Milner cried, throwing his arms around the narrow shoulders. "How are you, baby?"

Freddie's right eye started to mist. I looked down at my shoes, and the chief of staff cleared his throat. The Rock grunted and shifted his feet nervously.

"Baby, I was so worried. We about killed ourselves hurrying to your bedside. What's wrong with your chin?" He let go of the shoulders and turned frantically toward the doctor. "It won't disfigure him, will it?"

"No, it's going to be fine in a few days. Nothing serious."

Milner sighed, grabbing Freddie again. "What happened?"

Freddie shook his blond head sadly, a curl dropping across his brow. "I don't know," he said, and I was sure I detected a sob in his throat. "It happened so quickly. I was driving along and suddenly the brakes gave out. There was a sharp curve and—" He stopped and passed a hand over his face. "I couldn't make it. The car went out of control and flipped over." He looked across at the doctor and batted his good eye a couple times. "The car caught fire."

"Fire!" Milner gasped, his eyes popping out of his head.

Freddie nodded. "I was thrown clear on the first roll."

"Jesus, Jesus, Jesus," Milner chanted, running his hands over Freddie's bony knees. "Feel okay? Nothing broken? You sure, baby? You don't feel any pain in your back or legs anywhere?"

Freddie pushed his hands away. "I'm okay, Gus. I'm fine."

The doctor cleared his throat again and moved slightly forward. He, too, was a tall and cadaverously thin man, but the resemblance to Freddie stopped there. He had a hawk nose and a brilliant bald head. "Mr. Sharpe is a very lucky man," he said, pursing his bloodless lips. "A very, very lucky man."

"Somebody up there likes me," Freddie said, raising his eyes to the ceiling, without cracking a smile.

The doctor nodded his agreement. "Unfortunately, the young lady wasn't as fortunate."

Milner stood stock-still, his gray skin frozen into clay. "What young lady?" he croaked.

"Miss Adela Adams," the doctor said, looking down at Freddie.

"Well, for God's sake, tell me," Milner screamed. "What happened to her?"

"She was trapped in the burning car and severely burned."

"Oh, sweetheart," Milner said, embracing Freddie. "I don't even want to think about it. It's too horrible."

Freddie allowed Milner the privilege of comforting him. Neither spoke for a long time. Finally, I broke in with a question.

"How serious is it with the girl?"

"She'll live, but it will take a long time before she's well enough to leave the hospital."

"Will she be scarred permanently?"

"It doesn't look too hopeful. She received third-degree burns on her shoulders and the back of her head. Skin grafting will take care of her shoulders, but I doubt if the hair at the base of her skull will ever grow again. I believe the hair cells were destroyed. Of course, only time can tell us the true story."

"How much time?"

"A year. Maybe more."

"Do all you can for her, Doc," Milner said. "Don't worry about anything. We'll take care of the bill. Give her the best. Right, Freddie?"

Freddie nodded sadly. "Poor little kook," he said. "She was a good-looking chick. I hope she makes it all the way."

"We're fortunate in one thing," the doctor said. "She's very young and healthy. She should respond well to treatment."

I tried to remember what Marsha had said about Adela Adams. That was the kid from Nebraska that Phemie White was trying to make. Marsha had placed her age at sixteen.

"How young?" I inquired.

The doctor scratched his bald dome. "Sixteen, seventeen."

"You're crazy," Milner said, weakly protesting, slowly dropping his head to stare at Freddie.

"She's at least nineteen," Freddie said. "What the hell do you think I am? A cradle robber? And besides, it was strictly business. I had to come up to the Springs and she rode up with me so we could rehearse a scene coming up Monday."

"Well, I can be wrong, of course," the doctor said.

"That's right," Milner said. "These girls look a lot younger than they actually are. They always do in Hollywood. We've got fifty-year-old movie stars who don't look a day over twenty-five."

It was obvious that the doctor didn't want an argument. He nodded his assent and sat down. Slowly, word by word, the story unfolded. Some of the words came from Freddie, some from the doctor, and the rest from the Palm Springs police. They were very co-operative and duly impressed.

Later, at a downtown garage where the remains of Freddie's Maserati were being examined, I talked to a lieutenant who understood the situation perfectly.

"It was a terrible accident," he said, chewing on a thick wad of gum. "Could have happened to anyone. Too bad about the girl, but she would have been burned even if he had gone in after her. The guy was in a state of shock. Didn't know what was coming off."

The lieutenant was trying like hell to rationalize the fact that Freddie had done nothing to help the girl from the burning car. Instead he had hotfooted it down the road, holding his bleeding chin in his hand and screaming like a wild man. Adela Adams had saved herself by crawling out of the car and rolling on the sandy ground. It was the lieutenant's opinion that she would have suffered burns no matter what Freddie had done. In fact, by running down the road he had been able to summon help and had very probably saved her life.

I watched the lieutenant while he talked, wondering whether he really believed what he was spouting. I suppose if you try hard enough you can prove a point from any direction—to yourself, that is.

"What happened to the brakes?" I asked, walking toward the car.

"Just gave out," he said. "Line or master cylinder probably broke."

"Has the mechanic checked it out yet?"

"What difference would that make?"

"Aren't you curious?"

He laughed, shaking his head. "Listen, fella, if you'd seen as many accidents as I have, you'd stop being curious. Mr. Sharpe says his brakes gave out, and that's good enough for us."

"Humor me, Lieutenant. Get the mechanic to check them out."

"What's your angle, anyway?"

"Relax, Lieutenant. I'm on his side, too. Remember, I work for the man."

"Well, then, why all the questions? I don't get it."

"Look at it this way," I said. "This is a fifteen-thousand-dollar jalopy. If the brake line was defective, we'd like to know about it. Wouldn't you? This information will be strictly off the record."

The lieutenant gave the wad of gum a vigorous going over. "Okay," he said. "Off the record."

"That's right," I said. "Especially if there's nothing wrong with the brakes."

His small eyes hardened and narrowed to slits. "You sound to me like a man looking for trouble," he said, shifting the gum from cheek to cheek with the tip of his tongue.

"Lieutenant, I'm getting goddam tired of carrying you around this dance floor. I want to have that brake line checked, and I want it checked now. Do you hear me, Lieutenant? Am I coming in loud and clear?"

I had him pegged correctly. This was the only attitude he understood. You had to crack him across the knuckles a few times before he straightened up and wagged his tail like a good little puppy. He gave me one last defiant glare and obediently called the mechanic over to check the brakes. Even without the fire, the car would have been a total wreck. It had rolled over six or seven times from a speed of about ninety miles an hour. The Maserati is a low-slung super deluxe job from Italy, built for high-speed racing, as sensitive and high-strung as a blooded race horse, and a million times as dangerous in the hands of an amateur. I leaned forward, bending my knees, to look under the chassis as the mechanic wheeled himself under it. It didn't take him more than five minutes to locate the trouble.

"Here it is," he said, pointing with the beam of his flashlight.

I got down on my hands and knees, my head touching the greasy concrete, trying to see, but it was hopeless.

"Come on out," I said. "I want to use your creeper."

"That copper tubing broke about four inches from the fitting," he said, rolling out and standing up. "You're gonna ruin your good clothes under there."

"That's okay," I said. "It's on the swindle sheet."

I was sure I could still detect the cloying, sickening odor of burnt flesh as I pushed myself under. Oil dripped on my forehead and dirt fell in my eyes. The idea was to move without disturbing anything. I found the broken line, and it didn't take me long to see that it had received some help along the way. The line had been sawed halfway through, then held together by a small strip of black friction tape that had now slipped down the tubing. It was a crude job, but plenty effective. Now the question was whether I told the lieutenant or waited until I had talked it over with Milner and Sharpe. I decided to wait. I reached up and slid the tape from the tubing. Filching evidence is usually frowned upon by the police, but in this case I figured it would be safer in my pocket.

From the garage I drove back to the hospital, hoping to talk to Adela Adams, but they had knocked her out for the night. I drove back to Freddie's Palm Spring home. It wasn't as big as the one in Beverly Hills, but it was big enough to have satisfied J.P. Morgan. It was ranch style and painted a sedate pink. I drove up the circular asphalt drive and left the Caddy in front of the entrance.

Freddie looked better now. The doctor had given him a shot, and he seemed completely relaxed as he looked up at me from the white sofa he was lying on, fully dressed. Milner was standing at the foot of the sofa with a drink in his hand, his gray face creased with worry.

"Well, Vince, what did you find?" Milner asked.

I went to the coffee table and fixed myself a drink. "You can stop wondering about whether that crackpot means business," I said, looking directly at Freddie. "He does."

Freddie's serene expression didn't change. "Let's have the details," he said.

"The brake line was sawed through by someone who definitely wanted to see you dead. He missed this time only because you're a very lucky guy."

"Why a he?" he said, grinning at me.

Why a he, indeed, I thought. His popularity did not extend to men only. "You've got a point there," I said. "Which reminds me. How do you square this deal with the girl? Must cost a lot of money. She's badly burned. She might sue..."

"Don't worry about that end of it," Milner said. "What we need now is a hundred per cent protection for Freddie. Sweetheart, we're placing a big responsibility on your shoulders. You've got to keep America's number-one idol safe from harm of any kind."

"How about the police?"

Freddie waved his arms impatiently. "No coppers. And no publicity. The cops are going to sit on the press here. Nobody is gonna learn a thing about this accident if we can help it."

"You're forgetting one thing," I said. "A girl was badly injured tonight, and it wasn't an accident. You keep this information from the police and we all become accessories after the fact. That's a pretty steep charge."

"I can handle it," he said, snapping his fingers.

"Maybe you can, but I can't."

"Now, Vince, sweetheart, just give Freddie a chance to catch his second wind. He's been through a rough experience tonight. And besides, it's not our job to tell the police anything. If they can't find it out by looking at the car, why should we tell them? It's their job."

"Maybe it is their job. But at the moment they don't have the slightest reason to suspect foul play."

"Okay, then, sweetheart, let's leave it that way."

"But what about the girl?"

"I know, I know, Vince," Milner said, shifting nervously, the ice in his drink tinkling against the glass.

I turned to Freddie. "Doesn't she mean anything to you?"

He shrugged his shoulders. "She's a kook, but nothing special."

"What's a kook?"

"A screwball, but nice, you know."

"Nice and young, too."

"For Christ's sake, flip the record. What's the matter, are you some goddam social worker or something?"

"Now, now, sweethearts, don't fight. It's not important. The important thing is to get Freddie back to Beverly Hills before the news of the accident leaks out to the press. Christ, they'll fall on us like a swarm of locusts."

The Rock came into the room and tried to ignore me. I guess he had heard about the Killer and didn't like it much. He was a tough-looking Italian, with a pock-marked, olive-skinned complexion. He wasn't over five ten in height, but what he lacked vertically he more than made up horizontally. He was built like a steel box. From his shoulders to his hips, he was all one dimension, and without an ounce of loose fat. He was a shorter edition of the Killer, but younger, and maybe tougher. He didn't impress me as the sort who cared a damn about the rules of the New York Boxing Commission.

By this time it was nearly four o'clock, and I had had it for the day. "Well, if we're going back to L.A., let's go."

Milner winked at me, pleased that I had dropped the argument.

"The Rock will drive you and Freddie back. I have to stay and get things straightened out. I'll fly back in the morning."

It figured. Milner was the right guy for the mop-up operation. It was easy to see why he had lasted this long on the job. A neat guy like that was worth his weight in uranium to a messy guy like Freddie.

The ride back was a lot slower than the ride up. Freddie wasn't in any mood for racing. The Rock had it up over sixty once, but Freddie quickly discouraged him. Later, when I thought he was asleep, he softly posed a question in the darkness, not to me, but to the world in general.

"Why should anyone want to kill me? After all I've done for them." He lapsed back into silence, and I pondered that one awhile.

"Who's them?" I said.

He giggled. I guess that was a pretty potent sedative the doc had given him.

"The whole sad mess," he said. "All those stupid bastards."

"I suppose you mean the world," I said.

"Find him," he said. "Find the mother-lover. I want to spit in his ugly face."

"Why?" I said. "Because he hurt the girl or because he wrecked your beautiful car and spoiled your evening?"

He turned his head and stared at me with his one good eye. It was very black and very bright. "Don't overextend yourself, shamus. You're not indispensable."

I laughed. "Freddie, you're a very funny little man."

"Ah, screw you, you dumb schmuck."

"Well," I said. "If you'll keep your eye on the Rock, I'll catch forty winks." I saw the Rock's thick neck stiffen, but his head didn't move.

"What's that supposed to mean?" Freddie demanded.

"It means that from now on we don't trust anybody, except you and me. Everyone is suspect."

"Ah, you're nuts," he said, but his voice did not carry the conviction of his words. That one had gotten to him, real deep.

I slept the rest of the way.

7

BACK ON the Hilltop, I left the connecting door open to Freddie's room and locked both bedroom doors. Freddie didn't voice any objection to the security measures. He sat up in the king-size bed and watched me as I carefully checked the windows, drawing the drapes. I'd figured Freddie for a young thirty-seven, but he looked an old fifty-seven when I tucked him in that morning. Worry can do that to a man, especially to a man not used to worry. Despite his griping, Freddie had had it easy for a long, long time. Even early in his career as a singer, he had been a hell of a lot better off than I'd ever be. But that's not the way Hollywood looks at it. Once you get up to a million a year, you look back on the lean years and wonder how you ever survived. A hundred grand per is destitution. Fifty grand can only mean skid row.

In all probability, Freddie had been a despot of various magnitudes for nearly two decades. He was used to having people bow and scrape, prostrating themselves at his feet. When he told someone to jump, there was no argument, the only question was how high.

Now, all of a sudden, someone had tried to murder him, and he couldn't understand it. The idea was preposterous, beyond his comprehension. Why should anyone possibly want to harm him? He was Freddie Sharpe, the idol of millions, the secret passion, the hungering desire, the illicit dream of all womanhood. People of all ages, sex, color and creed stood patiently for hours on street corners and in long lines just for the privilege of gazing at him and, perhaps, if lucky, of touching his coat-sleeve.

To his way of thinking, the murderer had to be a psycho. The kind you read about in the papers every day. Killing just for kicks. It couldn't be anyone close to him. He was convinced that everybody loved him. I wondered what he would say when I told him my ideas on the subject. As far as I was concerned, the murderer had to be someone connected with his personal or household staff. Someone who had access to the garage. Sawing through that brake line wasn't a big job, not in time or skill. The only big thing about it was getting to do it without being seen. That took split-second timing and a lot of guts, twisted or otherwise.

Sleep eluded me for a long time. There was a lot on my mind, too much to let me sleep but not enough to give me any kind of satisfaction. All kinds of suspicious faces floated across my closed eyelids, grinning slyly before fading into that black pit behind my eyeballs. Finally I went to sleep.

I awoke with a start and sat straight up in the bed. I couldn't remember any dream, but I knew I'd had a real dinger. I stared confusedly at my watch, trying to decipher the hands. They were standing as close together as lovers on Mulholland drive. It was high noon. Slowly, I slid out of the bed and tiptoed into Freddie's room. He lay spread-eagled on his back, completely uncovered, the lavender silk pajama legs rolled up to his bony knees. His mouth was open, and his bruised eye reflected shades of yellow, green and purple. It was a colorful and touching scene.

I went back to my room and spent a good fifteen minutes under a cold shower. Then I went to the closet and gazed at my freshly pressed wardrobe. I decided to make it a gray day in honor of Milner's complexion. That's the way I felt. I selected charcoal worsted slacks, white oxford shirt, narrow black knit tie, gray tweed jacket. To complete the ensemble, I retrieved the .38 special from the night stand and broke it open, spinning the cylinder. It was fully loaded except for the one empty cartridge. I closed it and dropped the hammer on the empty. Now it was ready for action the moment I touched the hair trigger. I slammed it into the belt holster at my side and buttoned the jacket over it.

After taking another peek at Freddie, I left the room, carefully locking the door after me. It was too late for breakfast and too early for lunch. I decided on a compromise. Steak and eggs, plus a gallon of coffee. The dining room was empty except for a couple of dames sipping coffee. I noticed that they began whispering the moment they spotted me, but I did my best to ignore them. That's quite a feat for me, especially when the dames are young and bursting out of their brief play togs. There was a hell of a lot of bare flesh winking at me under that table. I attacked the steak with the gusto of a starved tiger and nearly leaped on top of the table. I had forgotten about my aching jaw. I remembered the Killer quickly enough. I wondered how he was faring this morning. Worse than me, I hoped.

I was on my fourth cup of coffee when Gus Milner joined me at the table. If possible, his face was even grayer and his pinched nose more twitching.

"Sweetheart," he cried, brandishing a copy of the *Tribune* in front of my nose. "Have you seen the morning paper? Man, we're sunk. All the way down to the bottom."

"Are you including me in that sinking?"

"Sweetheart, we're all going down with the ship. Look at this." And he opened the paper and gave me a quick glance at the banner headline before waving it away again. That was all I needed to see to know what he meant. The headline read: *SHARPE RECEIVES DEATH THREAT,* and the subhead had me tagged along with it: HIRES PRIVATE EYE FOR PROTECTION.

"Let me see that," I said, grabbing the paper out of his shaking hands. I read the first two paragraphs and gave it back to him. "They know it all, Gus."

"You're telling me? They don't only know how many notes there were, they even know the exact wording. Vince, I don't get it. Not more than four or five people knew this information. How the hell did they get it?"

"I don't know, but it will be interesting to find out," I said, pushing back my chair and standing up. "You're going to be around for a while?"

"Unfortunately. I'm going into the lion's den right now. If the roof flies off, you'll know why."

I did a double take on that one, surprised at the edge of sarcasm in his tone. But he was smiling, his fingers pinching the nostrils.

"For a moment there I thought you had joined the rest of the claque."

"Claque?"

"What else?" I said, and left him with his gray face perplexed.

The first one on my list was Marsha. I found her in Freddie's private office, sitting behind Freddie's walnut desk, looking very much like a personal secretary. She wore a light green silk suit and long dangling emerald earrings—simulated, I presumed. But then, you can't ever tell in Hollywood. Some of these dames go to work in mink. She looked up when I came in and gave me a frigid stare.

"Making like a secretary, I see. It's almost becoming."

"I've no time for B.S. Say it and blow, shamus."

What is that they say about a woman scorned? I sat down and regarded her, sans smile. "Well, to tell you the truth, I was sort of hoping for a re-match. We were going great there for a while."

"I'm busy."

"Oh, I see. Well, that's too bad. Some other time."

"You bastard," she said. "You've had it."

I sighed deeply. "Read the paper yet?"

"I know what you're going to say. I had nothing to do with it."

"Come again. Slower this time."

"Go to hell."

"What does your intuition tell you this morning?"

"It tells me that you're a sonofabitch."

"Such language," I said.

"Oh, you lousy bastard."

"Cut it," I said, lowering my voice an octave. "And tell me why you spilled the story to the press. How much was the payoff?"

Her jaw dropped and I thought she was going to throw something. "I told you the truth, goddammit."

"And I told you I don't believe you. Besides the two of us, only three other persons knew about this—Goldman, Sharpe and Milner. It's a sure bet they didn't tell the press. That leaves you and me. And I know about me."

Her face contorted angrily. "You're a real smart bastard, aren't you? One, two, three—and bingo. Just like that, and you've got the answer. Go to hell."

"It won't take Freddie long to arrive at the same answer."

"He can go to hell, too."

"That's not nice. After all he's done for you, you oughta be ashamed."

"Get out of here," she cried. "You make me sick."

"I affect a lot of people that way. It's occupational."

She fumbled with a pack of cigarettes and finally managed to light one. She blew a cloud of smoke in my direction that would have sheltered a convoy. "You're just plain disgusting," she said. "The best thing you can do is leave here. Who needs you?"

"Let's not get confused," I said, folding my arms behind my head. "I'm not here to discuss my virtues, as plentiful as they may be. Let's try to stick to the subject. Tell me what I want to know, and I'll be on my way."

"I told you, goddammit. It was just a wild guess when I said that to Freddie. I was just being my usual clever self. Why can't you understand that? I'm always saying clever things. It's expected of me. It's part of my job. I have more clever repartee than Chauncey has pratfalls."

Finally, she was coming around the barn. "Listen, kid," I said, assuming a confidential tone. "Nobody is going to spank you if you told the press. That's not the important thing."

"No?"

"No. Tell me that you did, if you did, and that's the last you'll ever hear of it. I give you my word."

"I told you the truth. I didn't leak it to the papers."

"Okay, then, maybe you know who did."

"I don't."

"How many people do you suppose knew about the threats?"

Her mouth opened and closed and nothing came out. Finally she picked up a pile of papers on her desk and started shuffling through them. "No one that I know of," she said, her attention on the papers.

"Okay," I said. "But remember, that kind of attitude works two ways. Before this little party is over, you may wish you had a friend." I stood up and got the hell out. She needed time to think that one over in privacy.

8

I F A hunch is strong enough, I listen to it. More often than not it's the only thing I have going for me. I'm not the jig-saw type of detective. I don't go sniffing around for clues, hoping to find a speck of dust for the lab or an old match folder, complete with name and address of the villain's last hermitage. I guess that type of detection is okay if you've got plenty of cerebral power and time. Anyway, according to some psychiatrists, hunches, when applied to a person's business, are usually based on subconscious deductions. If that's so, then I'm in fairly good shape. I've played a hell of a lot of them in my time, and brought home some real kickers.

At this moment, the release of the story to the *Tribune* kept nagging at me. I knew I wouldn't feel right until I checked it out. In itself, it didn't seem to have much value. And yet I felt it had a direct connection with the threats.

So, instead of questioning the members of the claque, I decided to get the information direct from the horse's mouth. This particular horse happened to be an old buddy of mine. I had known Murray Smith, city editor of the *Tribune,* in the old days when he had had nothing better to do than hang around Vice, killing time between deadlines, waiting for that big one to break his way. We played a lot of pinocle in those days, and you can't play too much pinocle with a guy unless you like him as a man. The feeling, I knew, was mutual. In recent years I had tossed a number of exclusive yarns his way. Now I hoped he would throw one my way.

I noticed as I came down the hill that the number of guards at the gate had been increased to five. I stopped and waited while one of them sauntered up to the car.

"Is this trip necessary?" he asked, grinning sheepishly.

I could hear the racket on the other side of the wall. "Why? Being attacked?"

"Man, those crazy bastards are ready to climb the wall. Every reporter in California is out there, just waiting for us to open that gate."

"Well, chief, I hate to tell you this, but it is necessary."

"Jesus! I need some reinforcement."

"How about my running over them? Think it would help?"

"I'd like to throw a grenade over there. Just one little pineapple. Bang! I'd make mincemeat of the whole goddam bunch."

This guy sounded like my old Marine sergeant. There was nothing that gyrene liked better than blowing up somebody's guts in a fine spray.

"Hate to spoil your siesta, chum, but open them pearly gates. I'm coming through."

"Christ! I could've made a C-note for that. Now it's for free."

"Wait a minute," I said. "You boys better get on the ball and keep those reporters on the outside."

"With what?" he asked. "I don't even have a club."

I was getting tired of him. "That's your problem," I said. "Just open the goddam gate."

The slight smile faded and the eyes hardened. "Yes, sir," he said, biting real hard on the "sir." He spun around and swaggered toward his buddies for a quick huddle. A couple of heads turned to give me hard looks, but they finally opened the gate. I blasted the horn and goosed the engine, leaving it in neutral, hoping that the noise would spook the reporters out of the way. It did. Not for long, but long enough for me to barrel through the shouting, milling crowd. A couple of flash bulbs exploded and I got the hell out of there in a hurry.

First I heard the shrill screech of a siren, then the powerful roar of an engine. I wrenched the Ford into the bushes, stomping on the brake just a split second before a black police limousine came careening around a curve, slipping completely across the solid white line. The brass huddled in that backseat nearly blinded me. I guess even hard-boiled city cops can't resist an opportunity to hobnob with a movie star.

I came out of the hills and took Sunset to the Hollywood freeway. The *Tribune* was in the Civic Center, close to City Hall— and in more ways than one. I left the Ford at one of those larcenous parking lots, which advertise fifty-cent parking in two-foot type and the fact that it's only for half an hour in agate type.

It was a few minutes after two when I walked into the City Room. Murray Smith was relaxing with a cup of coffee. It was between deadlines, and about every guy in the room was either gassing or reading the paper. One character had his feet up on the desk, a sandwich in one hand and a paperback novel in the other. A real informal atmosphere.

Murray winked when he saw me and patted an empty chair next to him.

"Rest the frame, boy," he said, in his slow, lazy way. "Want some coffee?"

"If it's not too much trouble."

"No trouble at all," he said, snapping his fingers above his head. "Still barbarian?"

"Right."

A copy boy ran up to the desk and Murray ordered it black.

"Had you on the front page today, fella. Old Murray's always there looking out for your interest. Spelled your name right, too."

"If things ever slow down and I need a press agent, you're my man."

"You could do worse."

"Not at the moment."

"Oh. Something wrong?"

"You might say that."

"Just tell old Murray," he said, reaching for a pencil and paper. "Okay, lay it out, boy." He laughed and dropped the pencil. The copy boy returned, still running, with the coffee.

"Who's that? Sammy?"

"Good boy. Best coffee fetcher I've ever had. Can't spell worth a damn, but man can he run. Be great for Western Union."

I leaned back in the chair and tasted the coffee, grimacing.

"Delicious, heh?"

"Yeah. Troop-ship brand."

He lit a cigarette and turned in the chair to face me. "How's the action at Sharpe's?"

"Not so good right now. That story of yours didn't help the situation."

"Sorry, Vince, but it's news."

"Yeah, and it can be murder, too."

"That sounds serious."

"Dammit, Murray, you know the score in these deals. If that joker is a psycho this story can trigger him off. He'll be forced by ego alone to make the threat good."

"Hey, now. Take it slow. It's not that bad."

"The hell it isn't."

He regarded me calmly for a long time, then shook his head. "You mean to tell me you don't know the source of this story?"

"Hell, no. But I sure as hell want to find out."

"Somebody is sucking you in, fella. I'm surprised."

"Never mind how surprised you are, just tell me."

"I knew it was a cooked-up deal. But it sells papers."

"For Christ's sake, Murray, spill it."

"Simmer down, boy."

I glared at him and suddenly realized how worked up I was getting, and for nothing. Murray would tell me, but in his own sweet time. I tapped his arm and smiled. "Sorry, friend."

"Forget it. I know you, fella. This thing's got you on the ropes. That's all."

"How's the wife and kids?" I could be as civilized as the next guy.

He laughed, slapping the desk top. "That's more like the old Vince. Everybody's fine. Jimmy's going to Stanford in the Fall. You ought to see him. Almost as tall as you are. Made all-conference fullback last year."

"That's swell," I said, and sincerely meant it. I hadn't seen Jimmy in over two years. He had been a skinny boy then. "What have you been feeding him?"

"Everything. He's a human garbage disposal. Eats anything that won't eat him first."

"Football scholarship?"

Murray nodded. "Marty Lewis gave me the story," he said.

Just like that. That was Murray's way. I didn't even bat an eyelash. There was no way for me to have known that, and yet I wasn't the least surprised. "What do you know about Lewis?"

"Typical Hollywood hotshot promoter. Full of bandini. Ratty little bastard, if you know what I mean."

"I know exactly what you mean."

"As far as I can gather, he started out promoting beauty queens. Had more big tits under contract than Minsky. Not one ever made it even small. But they all clocked plenty of mileage on the old casting couch. Well, you know the route. Lewis was just a high-class pimp. Whenever a director got hot flashes, Marty provided him with a cool dip—size and color of his choice. The poor stupid girls didn't know which side was up. They thought they were screwing their way to fame. Fame, hell! After a year or so, everybody on the circuit got tired of their face and rump, and they found themselves on the street, doing what came most naturally to earn a buck. Lewis, in the meantime, was out there, scouting the beauty contests, procuring and promoting newer and bigger tits."

I didn't say a thing. His words reminded me of Charlie. Poor old Charlie with the monkey on her back. Charlie was my wife, or rather, had been my wife until the night I found her in my bed with a guy by the name of Joey Strollo. At that time, Strollo was a petty hoodlum with a big ambition. In those days he dabbled in prostitution, narcotics and gambling. Later on he controlled big portions of each. He probably would have gone all the way to the top if it hadn't been for his twisted hoodlum ego. For four years he dreamed of revenge against me, savoring the most sadistic types of mayhem his sick mind could conjure. I had mangled his arm for keeps the night I caught him with Charlie. One week later he had me kicked off the police force. Charlie and I were divorced after that, and she disappeared into that twilight world of junkies. Strollo continued to prosper, becoming a favored son in the Mafia. His name became a household dirty word. Then one night, four years later, he tried to kill me, and when that failed he tried to frame me for murder. No need to go into those details now. Suffice it to say that Joey Strollo is presently sweating it out in death row at Quentin. Charlie is at Lexington, trying for what will probably be her last chance to kick the habit.

I knew about guys like Lewis. He wasn't Strollo, but in his own dirty way he was just as destructive. That hunch of mine had paid off. Maybe not a very big payoff, but every little bit counts.

I stood up and placed a hand on Murray's shoulder. "Thanks, friend. If something big breaks, you'll get it first as usual."

"Well, Vince, there's something you could help me with right now."

"Name it."

"Sit down," he said, and waited until I was back in the chair before going on. "Heard Sharpe was in an accident last night, or probably early this morning. We're having a hell of a hard time getting any specific information on the story. It seems the Palm Springs police are keeping the lid on. Harry Goldman stepped right into the middle of it, and that sonofabitch plays a hell of a tight game. I understand there was a girl in the car with Sharpe. The rumor is she's dead. How about it, Vince?"

That was a tough one. I owed Murray something for his confidence, and I owed Goldman and Sharpe something for their money.

"I know about it," I said. "But I can't tell you right now, Murray. I will tell you one thing, though. Nobody died."

He stroked his chin and lit another cigarette. "Tell me this. Any connection with the threats?"

"I don't know."

"Well, actually, I think it's just one hell of a coincidence. That other business is just a phony publicity stunt. I've seen a million of them. And this particular one more than once."

I was getting anxious to talk to Marty Lewis. I stood up again. "Got to get moving, Murray. Thanks for everything. I'll let you know as soon as I can."

Murray didn't press me, and I was thankful. We shook hands and I left. I didn't waste any time getting back to the Hilltop. The crowd of reporters had thinned out to half a dozen, and I recognized two or three of them.

"Hey, Vince," one of them called when I stopped before the gate. "What gives here, man?"

"Nothing right now. Everything is under control."

"Slader," another one asked, pushing his way to the car. "Gonna kiss Joey good-by next month at Quentin?"

I tapped the horn. What the hell can you say to a question like that? Some reporter.

The gate swung open and I drove in, the character still holding onto my door, running beside the car, his fat face red and grinning. One of the guards caught him as I went through the gate. "You sonofabitch," I muttered, getting a glimpse of him in my rear-view mirror, "you'll never know a goddam thing, but I'd sure love trying to teach you something, the hard way."

I avoided the screwballs cavorting in the living room and went directly to Marty Lewis's private foxhole.

9

HE WAS on the phone again, his feet up on the desk and his small head cocked to one side, the receiver cradled in his shoulder as he clipped his nails. His eyebrows came up when I entered, and his feet hit the floor with a bang when I locked the door behind me.

"What the hell," he croaked, cupping his hand over the mouthpiece. "Unlock that door."

I didn't say a word. I just reached over and pressed down on the cradle, cutting off his call. Then I sat on the edge of the desk and leaned forward until my face wasn't more than six inches from his long spindly nose.

"What do you hear from the *Trib,* Marty?"

"What's coming off here," he whined, pushing back his chair. He didn't go very far before he hit the wall.

"Marty," I said. "We're going to have a nice long heart-to-heart talk. The kind you use to have with your daddy when you were just a little shaver. And if you don't level with me, I might just spank you like a good daddy should. Get it, son?"

"You're crazy," he said.

"And you're very original," I said. "Always there with a snappy answer." The fear in his eyes was almost pathetic. I knew what he was afraid of, and it didn't have much to do with my muscles.

"I don't get it, Slader. Why-why-why lock the door?"

"I didn't know you stuttered. Thought you were a real sharp operator."

"I don't stutter."

"Good," I said. "What I'm looking for right now is a man who can talk without any handicap."

"Talk about what?"

I gripped his knee and pulled his chair up so that we were intimate again. "Marty," I said. "I want the full story."

"What story?"

"And I don't want to work for it, either. Start at the beginning and go right to the end. Understand?"

"You're trying to con me into something," he said.

I remembered what Murray had said about all those big tits, and I let him have one on the side of the head with the palm of my hand. His beady eyes blinked like the lights of a tilted pinball machine.

"Ouch," he cried, holding his head in both hands.

"No more horsing around," I said, raising my hand again. It was a rough way to do it, but I don't have much sympathy for little rats like Lewis. I've known too many of them.

He tried to duck the blow and nearly fell out of the chair. I held back my hand. "Just had a long talk with Murray Smith," I said. "He's a good friend of mine. Told me something very interesting." I reached over and took hold of the front of his coat. "You either tell me now, sonny, or I'm going to bounce you against all four walls."

"Okay," he said. "So I called him and gave him the story. Jesus Christ. It's a good story. Look at all the free news space we got. All over the country. That space is worth millions of dollars. You just can't buy that kind of space, you know what I mean."

"You're doing fine," I said. "Just keep it up."

"Well, that's all there is to it."

"Where did you get the story?"

"I can't tell you that. It's privileged."

This time I really whacked him one. He nearly toppled over in the chair. When he regained his balance, he was bawling, the fat tears popping out of the corners of his beady eyes. "Only five people knew that story," I said. "You're number six. Where did you get it."

"Marsha told me," he said.

"Okay," I said. "Let's find out." I grabbed the phone and pressed the intercom button. "What's her number?"

"Wait, wait," he cried. "It's not true. It's a lie. She didn't tell me. Somebody else did."

"Who?"

"I can't tell you."

"You miserable little bastard," I said, shaking him, his head flopping on his shoulders. By this time, I was getting some pretty wild notions. "Nobody told you. Nobody had to. You knew it before anybody else did. You wrote those threatening notes yourself. Right?" And I shook him some more. It was crazy, but I knew I'd struck pay dirt right off. He wept like an old woman, the sobs thundering in his chest.

"It was just a gimmick," he cried, staring wild-eyed at me. "You've got to believe me. I was scared I'd lose my job and I dreamed the whole thing up. Look at all the free news space I got for him. Worth millions."

"Why did you wait so long to tell the press?"

"I was waiting for the right psychological moment. When they hired you to protect him I knew it was time to release it."

For a moment there I was going along with him. I had completely forgotten about the attempt on Freddie's life in Palm Springs. Now, all of a sudden, nothing made sense.

"It was more than a gimmick," I said. "You hated him and tried to kill him."

"No! Freddie is a sweet guy. Why should I want to kill him? Man, I've got the best job I ever had in my life. He pays me twenty grand a year. It was just a gimmick. That's all."

What he said made sense, and I went along with him. He didn't strike me as the killer type. He was a weasel, all right; but murder in my book requires a different kind of guts. Lewis was more the scavenger variety of *Homo sapiens.*

"How many people know about the threats?"

"Everybody here knew about it," he said. "I passed it along."

"Why?"

"I thought maybe they'd leak it to the press. But they didn't. So when you came along I knew it was time, and I did."

"Who's they?"

"The gang. Stone, Chauncey, Crosby, Fowler, everybody."

"Did they know you wrote the notes?"

"Hell, no. I just spread the rumor. I'll bet they didn't even know I was the one who told them."

"Well, they will now," I said. "You're just about to get a million dollars' worth of free news space yourself."

His face had been pale, but now it turned ashen. "You're not gonna tell Freddie," he cried. "He'll kill me. You don't know this guy. Jesus, man, you can't tell him. What difference can it make now?"

"Didn't you see the cops when they were here?"

"The cops? I didn't see anybody. I've been busy all morning."

"Well, friend, this is a police matter now. You'll have to explain it to them."

"Look, wait, look. You can't do that. You don't know Freddie. He—"

I left him with his mouth open and his eyes clouded with fear. I had heard all I wanted for the moment. I went to my room to do some thinking. The bottle of bourbon was still on the night stand, and there was a fresh bucket of ice. Someone had been in to make the bed and straighten out the room.

After fixing myself a drink, I sat down and tried to organize my thoughts. I could forget about the death threats now. They had no significance at all. Well, none that I could connect with the attempted murder. Could I have been mistaken about the brake line being deliberately cut? After all, I was looking for evidence to prove foul play. And when you look hard enough for something like that, you usually find it—real or imaginary. That was the crucial question. Had I jumped to the conclusion I wanted? Maybe it was an accident, just a wild coincidence as Murray Smith had suggested. Murray hadn't known the facts, but he had been able to see the possibility. You started out with a certain set of facts and a certain conclusion was almost inevitable. But eliminate just one of those facts, and the whole damn thing crumbled.

I got up and went to the closet to retrieve the piece of friction tape from my jacket pocket. I sat down again and carefully unrolled the tape. It was the only thing that kept me from completely changing my mind. The more I thought about it, the more in circles I went. Finally I said to hell with it.

I got up and changed into a sport shirt. I looked down at the .38 special in my belt holster and decided to take it off before going out to the patio. I would hardly have any use for it out there. The connecting door to Freddie's room was closed, and I knocked on it before looking in. It was empty. My next stop was the garage.

Even in Southern California, where the average working man usually owns two cars, a six-car garage is considered king-size, especially when it has six cars in it. This one had five; the sixth one, the Maserati, had been consigned to a scrap heap in Palm Springs.

The place looked empty when I first walked in. I stood and stared at the gleaming paint jobs lined up in a neat row for my inspection. There was a brand-new light-blue Cadillac station wagon, a red Ferrari sedan, a black Rolls Royce, a white XK-150S Jaguar and a steel-gray Aston Martin. At least seventy grand worth of precision machinery.

I heard a noise behind me and turned to be greeted by a short, fat Mexican with tight black curls and buck teeth almost as white as his spotless coveralls.

"*Señor,*" he said, his dark face wrinkling up painfully in something that was supposed to resemble a smile. "You looking for Juan?" These guys have to smile so often in this country that for many of them it has become a conditioned reflex.

"No," I said. "Just admiring Mr. Sharpe's stable."

"*Si,*" he laughed, waving at the cars. "Nice *caballos.*" "What's your favorite?" I asked.

He shook his head and stretched out his arms to embrace them all. "All *muy fino.*"

"Well," I said. "You're not only neat, you're a diplomat."

"*Si, si,*" he said. "Juan very neat. Keep place clean all the time."

"You the mechanic?" I asked, quickly introducing myself.

"*Si.*"

"What are your hours?"

"*Si?*"

"What time do you come to work in the morning and leave at night?"

"Eight in the morning and five at night. Six days a week. No work Sunday."

"Anybody here after five?"

"Just me."

"Notice anything unusual this morning?"

He shook his head, puzzled.

"Look," I said. "You keep this place spic and span all the time. See anything missing, or in the wrong place?"

"No." He shrugged his shoulders.

I looked around, wondering where he kept the creeper. Juan followed closely behind me as I crossed over to the workbench. I found the creeper under it, leaning against the wall.

.

"Is that the way you left it?"

His eyes flashed understandingly. "No, no, no. I turn it the other way, with the wheels out."

"Then you haven't used it this morning?"

"No."

"*Fino*," I said. "We're in business, my friend. Now, one more thing. Got any friction tape?"

"*Si, si.*" He quickly opened a drawer in the workbench and handed me a roll of black tape. I held up the short strip I had taken from the Masirati, trying to match the ends to the roll. The possibility was there, but I would need an expert with a microscope to tell me for certain.

"Here," I said. "Cut me a piece."

He pulled a jackknife from his pocket and used his thumb to flip open a blade as finely honed as a razor.

"Do you always use your knife to cut tape?" I asked, placing the pieces of tape in my pocket.

"No, *señor*. Sometimes I just tear it off like this," he said, demonstrating his method of tearing, which was no diferent than anyone else's.

I nodded. "Now look," I said, starting for the door. I'll be right back with my car to pick up that creeper. Don't touch it while I'm gone. Savvy?"

He shook his head in confusion, still grinning, and followed me outside.

I brought the Ford around quickly and backed it into the garage. Lifting the creeper by the wheel brackets, I gingerly placed it in the trunk. I had a friend at headquarters who would take it from here.

I locked the trunk and left the car in the parking lot. Then I went back to the house and out to the patio, which everyone insisted on calling a lanai.

10

FREDDIE WAS huddled in a basket chair, gesticulating as he read from a script, the adhesive plaster along his jawline startlingly white against his deeply tanned face. Phemie White and Carlton Stone, also holding scripts, sat facing him in chairs around a table. Milner stood behind Freddie's chair, and the Rock was stretched out in a chaise longue a few feet away to Freddie's left, his impassive, pock-marked face even more ugly in bright sunlight.

The place was crowded again with the usual dames in the bikinis and the guys ogling them around the pool. There was a lot of splashing and squealing. I flopped in a chaise longue and Milner hurried over, his gray face creasing in a worried smile.

"Where you been, sweetheart?"

"Investigating," I said. "How's Freddie feeling?"

"Not bad, considering. He took the news pretty good this morning. I guess he feels lucky on that Palm Springs thing. Nothing in the paper on that."

"Well," I said, "he won't feel so good when he hears my news."

He leaned toward me and I gave him a quick run-down of the Smith and Lewis interviews. The worried smile froze into a gray mask; only his hands were alive, clasping nervously together for a firm hold.

"Jesus, God," he gasped, when I had finished. "The man's an idiot. Jesus, sweet God. What do I do now?"

"It might not be a bad idea to let the cops handle it."

He waved the suggestion aside. "They were here while you were out. I can tell you right now, Freddie won't buy it. And besides, our hands are tied. Hell, we can't let the press know it was a stunt. Jesus, they'd crucify us. They'd never believe Freddie wasn't behind it. You don't know those vultures. They're all waiting for Freddie to slip, make one little mistake. Believe me, there's no love lost there. They've given Freddie a hard row to hoe. And Freddie, being the guy he is, spat on them every inch of the way. Nobody pushes Freddie around and gets away with it. This boy was brought up in the toughest section of Brooklyn. He knows people. Believe me, big people everywhere."

I didn't question the "people" reference. I had a pretty good idea who he meant. It was fairly common knowledge that Freddie was on speaking terms with the biggest hoods in the country—and out of the country, as far as that went. Charlie Lucky was no stranger to Freddie. In fact, a few years back some enterprising photographer had caught them together in a Naples nightclub, and the picture had made all the front pages in this country. It hadn't hurt Freddie's career; if anything, it had enhanced it.

"Well, that's up to you and Freddie," I said.

"Freddie will handle it, don't worry about that. Well, I guess that washes up the deal for you, though, sweetheart."

"How's that?"

"The thing was just a stunt. There's no danger now."

"Are you forgetting about the attempt last night?"

He scratched his bald head. "That must have been an accident."

"I don't think so," I said. "That line looked tampered with to me."

"You can't be sure about a thing like that," he said.

"That's right," I said. "Either way."

He dropped down on the edge of the chaise longue. "Might be wise to keep you on for a few days, just so the press don't get wise. But I better tell you one thing. The Killer is still pretty much steamed up about last night. Stay out of his way if you can, sweetheart."

"Give him a message for me," I said. "The next time he tries anything with me, I'm going to part his hair with a gun-sight."

"Take it easy," he said. "The Killer's okay. He don't mean no harm."

"I know. He's just a big playful elephant on a stampede."

"He's got a mean temper. Freddie is the only one who can really handle him. Well, after all, he's been with Freddie fourteen years. He's got a right to be sore. Anyway, I told him the whole story this morning. He still has his job. The big jerk actually thought he was getting the boot. No need to fake it now with the damn thing out on the front page and all."

I looked around the patio. "Tell me, Gus. Of all the people here, who has the best motive to kill Freddie?"

Gus looked startled. "What's this? It's just a gag, man."

"It's no gag," I said. "And last night was no accident."

Milner slowly stood up. "You're wrong, sweetheart. Everybody here loves Freddie."

"Okay," I said. "Have it your way, Gus."

"I don't like to hear things like murder," he said. "It makes me sick."

"It will make you a lot sicker if the murderer succeeds."

"Don't say that. Jesus, what a horrible thought."

I leaned back in the chaise longue and Milner went back to stand behind Freddie's chair. I had noticed during my talk with Milner that the Rock had kept glancing at me with more than a passing interest. Now as I stared at him his gaze wandered away, looking everywhere, as though he were interested in all things. I waited and it finally came back to me, quickly darting away the moment he saw I was still watching him. Then Freddie snapped his fingers—that famous snap his fans admired so much when he sang—and the Rock moved like greased lightning. A cigarette materialized from nowhere.

Freddie never even moved his head. The cigarette appeared between his lips and a flame glowed under it. All Freddie had to do was breathe. Man, that was service.

I returned my attention to the patio and selected candidate number one. Tiny Tim Crosby was lying with his head in the shapely lap of a redhead who must have been at least six inches taller than he was, barefoot. I beckoned a red-and-blue Filipino and told him to fetch me Mr. Tiny Tim.

Tiny Tim received the message, raised his head to look at me and promptly stood up, hurrying to my side.

"Want to see me?" he asked, standing there like a little kid again.

"Yeah, Tim. Sit down."

"Thanks," he said, looking me over closely before sitting on the edge of the chaise longue. "Congratulations. Hear you gave it real good to the goon. That bum had it coming for a long time. Everybody's pretty happy about it. You made a lot of friends last night."

"Well, I need friends, Tim. Has the Killer bothered you before?"

"He's a wise guy. Always flexing his muscles. About time he got a few lumps of his own."

"I understand Freddie likes him. Been with him fourteen years."

"Why not? It's like having one of them big ferocious dogs around. All Freddie has to say is 'get 'em, boy,' and that big goon is after you."

"Well, then, it's not really the Killer's fault. He just does what he's told."

"Yeah. I suppose so."

"Tell me something, Tim. Why does a guy with your talent stick around here?"

"Man, I make five bills a week."

"Couldn't you make more on the outside?"

"Maybe. If I could get a couple big hits."

"What do you think of those threatening notes?"

"I don't know. Maybe it's just a crank."

"Did you know about it before this morning?"

He looked me straight in the eye and shook his head. "Not a word. It was a blow, man."

"You think somebody here is sending them?"

He looked startled. "Here?"

"Yeah. Here."

"That's way out, man. Why should anybody here want to do that? Naw. It's just one of them poison-pen deals."

"How do you get along with Freddie?"

"Fine, man. The greatest. He's a sweet guy."

"He didn't sound so sweet yesterday afternoon."

His gaze hardened, but I couldn't tell whether it was because of the question or the memory. "That don't bug me none, man. I'm used to it."

"Then what were you bawling about?"

His small body stiffened and he started to get up. "Sit down," I said. "I'll tell you when you can leave."

He didn't question the order. He dropped back down and folded his hands in his lap. "You're taking the Killer's place, eh?"

"Not exactly. I'm here to discourage anyone who thinks he can murder Freddie and get away with it."

"I'm not trying to murder him. Man, I've got it made here. It's a great deal all around."

"There we go again," I said. "Shangri-La."

"You'll see, man. It's like stealing." Suddenly his face lit up. "Wow, man! Look who's making the scene."

I looked up, following his gaze, and caught Lisa Love making what is popularly known as an entrance. I had seen this dame in a number of movies, and each time she had made herself known to my adrenal glands. Now she was long-legging it across that patio like some colt filly running wild. All I could see at first was that long, swept-up black hair and dark flashing eyes. Later, after she got past me, I received the full treatment of that famous rump, now enclosed in skin-tight black capris. One is either too young or too old for that sort of thing. A stimulated adrenal is fine, but it can sure place a strain on that heart muscle, among other things.

Following in her erotic wake was Jeff Strong, a big hunk of male pulchritude as queer as a three-dollar bill. With him was a kid who looked like a thousand other starlets. Peroxide hair, thick red lips, a bust-line in the high thirties and hips like a boy. A perfect combination for all the latent homosexuals wielding power in the industry. They could enjoy the one while craving the other, all with the proper illusion.

"I'd cut it up to here, man," Tiny Tim said, slapping his shoulder. "For just one night with that sexpot."

"The line forms to your right," I said. "Who's the kid with Strong?"

"Who knows? Some kook."

Freddie finished reading his line before looking up from his script. He smiled, and Lisa leaned forward to kiss him, that delicious posterior secretly winking at me. Jeff Strong stepped in then, blocking the view, and proceeded to introduce the starlet. Stone stood up, but Freddie merely nodded. The starlet squirmed and fidgeted, and got more out of that nod than most dames get out of a tussle in the hay.

Suddenly Phemie White jumped up, the long cigarette holder bobbing between her lips. Milner stepped forward and took hold of her arm, his gray face intense as he talked to her, all the time trying to push her back down in the seat. Finally, she let herself drop, the holder clattering to the floor. She looked ill, on the verge of hysterics. I remembered what Marsha had said about her interest in Adela Adams. Evidently, she had just learned about the accident.

"Tiny," I said. "It was fun. See you around."

"Sure, dad. Next time you waltz with the Killer, give him a belt for me."

Tiny Tim left and I stood up, looking for a boy. I found one in the living room, and he escorted me to Matthew Fowler's room.

11

FOWLER LOOKED no more than thirty. He was a light-skinned, thin-featured Negro with oriental slanted green eyes and long black eyelashes. His thick curly hair was cropped down almost to his skull. He smiled, flashing a full set of pure-white teeth, and extended his hand. It was cold and wet, but firm.

"Come in, Mr. Slader. Here, take this chair. It's the most comfortable."

"Thanks," I said. The room was strewn with newspapers and magazines. "Doing homework?"

He smiled, flashing those good teeth again. "Always. Must keep up with a changing world."

"How long you been with Freddie?"

"Nearly two years."

"I understand you went to U.C.L.A."

"Yes." He sat on the bed, his back very erect.

"I did a stretch there myself."

He nodded. "It's a good school. Getting better all the time. Did you play football?"

"Some. Why? Do I strike you as the type?"

"Something like that."

I grinned. "You go in more for the intellectual approach."

"Oh, it's not that exactly. It's just that you look like you forgot to remove the shoulder pads after the last game."

The remark and the way he said it was more revealing than clever. This guy had very definite views on the subject, and it probably carried through to other unintellectual fields, such as singing and acting. "I understand you're Freddie's personal philosopher," I said, dismissing the shoulder-pad barb. "Must be a stimulating occupation."

"I don't mind it," he said. "The pay is quite satisfactory."

"So I've been hearing. Everybody around here is very happy with the economic situation. I can understand it with guys like Crosby and Stone, but I can't see it as the primary motivating force in your life's work."

The smile had slowly vanished from around his mouth, and now even his eyes became impassive. "Why not? Material things are just as important to me as they are to anyone else. I, too, have to eat."

"Guys interested in money don't usually go in for Ph.D.'s. Philosophers, the way I understand it, are more interested in philosophizing. Correct me if I'm wrong."

"The generalization is fair enough, as generalizations go. The point is that philosophers are also people, and as such they have differing viewpoints concerning values, materialistic or otherwise. I happen to be one of the practical ones. I enjoy the comforts of life. Can you blame me?"

"Hell, no," I said. "I do, too. To a point."

"After all, you know, a philosopher is somewhat of an anachronism in this age of engineering. About as useful as a toe dancer in a coal mine." Suddenly he stood up and walked to a small desk across the room. He turned and leaned against the desk, facing me. His green eyes had grown very dark. "When you're a nigger, you've got to take what you can. And—" he paused a moment—"be grateful."

His candid remark caught me unprepared. "I think you're selling short," I said. "Too soon."

"Maybe, but then how would you know?"

"True. I've just met you. I don't know what you have to offer. I've known a few worthless and useless Ph.D.'s in my time. I don't suppose it's a passport to success anymore, as being white is."

He ran his hands through his curly hair, slowly massaging his scalp, and suddenly smiled. "That's the trouble with my race," he said. "The ignorant ones gripe, the intelligent ones cry. It's a serious disease. Blaming one's social origin for failure has become a built-in rationalization. Too easy an escape."

"Well," I said. "What do you plan on doing about it?"

"Off the record," he said, "I've had an application in with the State Department for the last six months. I think I could be of some use there."

I nodded. Talking to this guy was interesting, but it wasn't getting me very far. "Look," I said. "I hate to change the subject, but there are a few questions I'd like to ask you."

"Certainly, go ahead."

"I assume you know why I'm here."

"I read the paper this morning."

"Was it a surprise to you?"

"You mean about the threatening notes?"

"Yeah."

"Not really. I had heard something about it earlier."

"From whom?"

"Just a rumor. It was more or less general knowledge."

"What's your opinion on it? Think somebody is really out to murder Freddie?"

His smooth features creased in concentration. "I don't have any more information than the paper, but I suppose it's a possibility. A man in Mr. Sharpe's position makes enemies along the way. I would judge it all depends on the kind of enemies."

"How about the kind that work for him, live right here?"

"I wouldn't know. I'm sure that's more along your line. You're the expert."

"I wish I were," I said, standing up. "Well, thanks for the conversation. Maybe we can get together again soon, and you can brief me on the world situation. I could use a briefing."

"It will be my pleasure." He moved away from the desk and followed me to the door, offering me his hand again.

"I wish I knew somebody in the State Department," I said, and left.

12

FREDDIE, GUS, the Rock and Phemie were gone when I got back to the patio. Lisa Love was still there with the rest of the group. Stone glanced up at me and winked.

"Everybody," he said. "This is Slader, our protector."

"Oh, the private eye I read about in the papers," Lisa said. "Christ, you're a big one."

Jeff Strong stood up then and offered me his hand, moving as close to me as possible. From the feel of the limp handshake, I knew he had something else in mind. He wanted Lisa to see that he had almost an inch on me.

"I'm Jeff Strong," he said. "I've read about you, too."

"I'm flattered," I said. "You're all much too kind."

Lisa laughed and held out her hand. I grabbed for it, leaning forward to peer at my reflection in her sparkling black eyes. I felt like some stage-struck kid. There are dames and broads, and then there are women. This was a *woman*. And she knew it better than anybody.

"Okay, Slader," Stone said. "You can let go of the hand now. I don't want you corrupting the morals of this fine young lady on her first day in the romantic land of make-believe."

The starlet giggled, and I slowly released Lisa's hand.

"I'm Janice Lang," the starlet said. "You can hold my hand if you like."

"Maybe later, when this ogre has gone back under his rock."

"Ogre, heh? Well, somebody around here has to safeguard the sanctity of the home. Remember, Slader, this innocent child probably has a mother. A poor mother who has selflessly sacrificed her own happiness to further her little girl's career. Picture, if you will, my dear Slader, this poor mother, sitting in an old rocking chair before the kitchen stove, silently spitting away her lungs in a king-size box of Kleenex, soulfully intoning a prayer to the blessed Virgin Mary. Would you want to violate this dear woman's innermost fears?"

"All writers are perverts," Lisa said.

"You are so right, my precious little pussy. How else could I write these sordid sexual catharses? Surely, not from the imagination."

"Yes, darling," she said. "Imagination is the last thing an actress expects from a screen writer."

"Excuse me for butting into the profound discussion," I said. "But what happened to Freddie and the others?"

Stone smiled slyly. "Phemie has flown to the bedside of her young love in Palm Springs. And Freddie is entertaining a dear old friend in his private office. I believe you know the gentleman. Mr. Nick Priziola, the renowned entrepreneur, the king of the juke boxes. Plus, of course, a couple of his young protégés, both equipped with cute little rods, nuzzled warmly against their bosom."

I nodded and headed for Freddie's office. Yes, I knew Nick Priziola, but in my book he was no gentleman. He was a fat slob who had murdered his way up to a top post in the Mafia. Priziola called himself the biggest man in the Mafia, and he was, physically. He weighed over four hundred pounds and stood no taller than five-six in his custom-made elevator shoes. His neck was thicker than Lisa Love's waistline.

I knocked on the door and went in without invitation. Nick was sitting behind Freddie's desk, pounding it with both fists, his monstrously huge body shaking with anger. It usually didn't take much to make Nick angry, and similarly it didn't take much to make him laugh. He had a very short emotional curve.

Freddie sat on the desk, listening to Nick, hugging his knees to his chest. Both the Rock and the Killer were sitting in chairs against the far wall. I ignored the Killer's dark brooding stare. Milner was standing between Phil Capolla and Jack Gizzo, two goons of the lowest order. Capolla was a tall, swarthy, pock-marked Sicilian with lifeless pale-blue eyes. He was Nick's number-one man, and he stuck so close to Nick that he was known as the fat man's thin shadow. Gizzo looked enough like Capolla to be his twin brother, except he had dull black eyes that reminded me of smoked glass. They were both known enforcers for the Mafia. Good company for a movie star.

Priziola's clean-shaven bullet head came up from between his bulging shoulders with the wary deliberation of a turtle. His eyes were black beads buried behind countless layers of fat, and his lips were thick and glistening wet. Huge diamonds sparkled from each of his little fingers, and his long fingernails were painted a rose pink. Even from where I stood, I could smell that whorehouse mixture of sweat and exotic perfume.

"Get lost, shamus," he croaked in his hoarse, wheezing bellow. "Talking business."

I looked at Freddie, and he waved his approval of Nick's order. "See you later, Slader. This is private."

"Sure," I said, turning to leave.

"Wait minute," Nick growled in his typical abbreviated English. "You take care my boy, good, understand? Something happen and Nick give you business, but good, understand? This boy—" and he slapped Freddie's leg—"is my friend. Understand?"

What else could I say? And so I did. "I understand," I said.

"Lousy fink," he cried, slapping the desk top again. "Nick don't forget Joey. Understand?"

"So," I said. "Don't forget. Who gives a damn?" There are limits even to what I can take, patient and understanding as I am.

"Smart bastard," he growled. "You get yours some day."

You could have shoveled and packaged the silence in that room as we stared at each other. It was that heavy. There was a lot of things I could have said in answer, but what good would they have done? The only sound a punk like Priziola hears is violence. And, unless you are willing to express it, you might as well keep your mouth shut.

Freddie broke the silence. "Better go, Slader," he said. "I'll see you when Nick leaves."

I nodded and got out, going directly to my room. I stretched out on the bed, folded my hands behind my head and waited for the anger to simmer down to a slow boil.

I've had enough contact with hoods to know something about their warped personalities. They are either psychotic or psychopathic. Their mode of living has been fully rationalized. Some are even prudish and righteous. It's very much like the crazy man who thinks the whole world is insane except himself. The professional hood thinks the whole world is corrupt. This is especially true of the Mafia. They have built a society within a society, where intermarriage is as solidly enforced as between Catholics, Jews and Negroes. It has become a self-perpetuated clan, growing in geometrical proportions. Unless something drastic is done soon, it will be the hood, and not the Communist, who will take over this country. They have already infiltrated every segment of business, labor and government. The threat is there for everyone to see, but no one seems to give a damn. Elections have been rigged before, and they will be rigged again, even on a national scale. How much choice is there between two Mafia candidates, one for each party? If a Bill O'Dwyer can become mayor of New York City, why can't he become governor or even president? The professional hoodlum has already paralyzed law-enforcement agencies, including the FBI. In thirty years' time, Los Angeles has had over sixty gangland slayings without a single conviction. Multiply this by every other big city in this country, and the sum total staggers the wildest imagination. And, as far as the FBI is concerned, they are much more adept at capturing a renegade like Dillinger than an Albert Anastasia.

Disgusted, I sat up in bed and reached for the bottle, taking it straight. To see a Nick Priziola, arrogant and successful, always turns my stomach. It's at such times that I'm glad I'm off the police force. Now I don't have to sit there and watch those punks literally get away with murder. I spent nine years on the Vice squad, poring over human garbage, most of it created by pigs like Priziola and Strollo. Dope, prostitution, gambling—every crime in the book. Nothing's too small, too big, too clean or too dirty to interest the *mafioso* if there's a buck in it.

I stood up and went into the bathroom, leaning against the sink to stare at my ugly puss. The wrinkles were not only getting more plentiful, they were getting deeper and longer. I was getting to look like the rock of ages. Lots of crags and fissures and grooves. A real old fossil. I ducked my head under the faucet. Maybe the cold water would clear up my thinking, get me back on the right track. My hair is dark and curly, but I keep it cut short. That way I can shower every day and not worry about hair oils. I moved away from the sink and grabbed blindly for a towel. A stimulating head rub is always good for the brain cells.

Back in the bedroom, I picked up the phone and dialed police headquarters. Frank Delaney, a sergeant on the Vice squad, had been an old buddy of mine since the war. We served in the Marine Corps together, and then joined the force at the same time. Frank was forty-three, a couple years my senior, married and with six kids, all carbon copies of himself. That boy had powerful genes.

Unlike the movie version of a cop, Frank had an unusually soft voice.

"Vince," he said. "Been reading about you. Up to your old tricks, heh?"

"Yeah," I said. "Probably get a screen test any day now."

"The hell with that," he said. "How are you making out with the dolls?"

"Great. I held Lisa Love's hand for all of thirty seconds."

"Lisa Love! Boy, that's for me. How about wrangling an intro?"

"Sure," I said. "Give me Helen's written permission and I'll fix you up."

Frank laughed. "You made your point, friend. What else is on your mind? Don't tell me this is just a social call."

"Yes, and no. First, how are Helen and the kids?"

"Oh, fine. Helen was asking about you. Wants you over to dinner. I do, too, Vince. How about coming over?"

I was touched. I really loved this guy, and it was nice to know that the feeling was mutual. "The very first chance I get, Frank. I can't right now, of course. I have to stay with this character twenty-four hours a day. But the minute this case breaks, I'll be over. You can count on that."

"Fine, I'll tell Helen. Now what's the business?"

Frank was a good listener. Being a cop helps develop that talent. I told him the whole story, not in detail, but touching all the high points. Frank was smart enough to fill in the rest.

"Be glad to do it, Vince," he said, when I got through. "I'll be over in a half-hour at the most."

"See you, buddy."

"Right," he said, and hung up.

There was a banging on the door, and I hurried to open it. Tiny Tim stood there, badly shaken, his eyes wide with terror.

"You better come," he cried. "They're in there, killing Marty."

"Who's in there?" I said, brushing past him.

"Those guys with Priziola. They're in Lewis's office, beating his brains out."

This was something I should have anticipated, and it made me mad to realize that I hadn't. I sprinted down the hall, with Crosby puffing behind me. Everybody in the living room had crowded near the door to Lewis's office, and I had to force my way through them. I wasn't any too gentle about it. There they stood, all of them, their mouths gaping open, their feet glued to the floor.

The door to Lewis's office was closed and locked. I stepped back and pounded my leather heel just under the knob, where it would do the most good. The lock wasn't a very good one; it quit with the first kick. The door flew open, slamming against the inside wall.

The picture that greeted my eyes was ugly, but very typical. Gizzo stood behind Lewis, his left arm snaked around Lewis's neck, pulling his head back, while his right hand held Lewis's arm in a hammer lock. Capolla stood in front of Lewis, his dark face set in a fixed grin, his black gloved fists pounding away at Lewis's frail body.

By the time the door slammed against the wall, I was on top of Capolla. My first blow caught him on the side of the head, and he went stumbling sideways, the fixed grin erased by an expression of startled anger.

I swung around, ready to deal with Gizzo, and found myself grappling with the limp body of Lewis, which Gizzo had thrown at me. Lewis clung desperately to me in his pain and blindness. The guy had been hurt enough without my tossing him aside. The dodge worked the way Gizzo had anticipated. I held on to Lewis and tried to drag him to his chair behind the desk. But we never made it. Gizzo fell on top of us, and the only thing I could see was the dull leather of the sap high above my head. I tried to duck, still holding on to Lewis. I don't know why I didn't let him drop. I guess I was afraid he would be trampled to death. Somthing solid and sharp slid down the side of my head, burying itself into the soft part of my shoulder. I swung my right arm, still holding Lewis with my left, and missed. The force behind the blow was so great that it sent me spinning across the room. I went down on my knees, and Lewis crumpled under my weight. I left him there.

I turned, still on my knees, and caught Gizzo's foot in my chest. Capolla was up and coming to Gizzo's aid.

Fighting two guys is always tough, but fighting two pros like Gizzo and Capolla can be suicide. Gizzo started another kick and I threw myself forward, my right arm swinging out under him, slamming hard against his left shin while his right leg was still in mid-air. There was a sharp growl as he flew backward and landed on his back, his head striking the desk.

The next second I was on my feet, rushing toward Capolla. I saw a knife flash in his hand, but it was too late to mean a damn thing. I feinted with a left and swung a right across that connected with the impact of a sledge hammer. His head snapped back and his eyes glazed. Capolla was through for the day. Knife and man clattered to the floor, one as inanimate as the other.

By this time Gizzo was halfway up from the floor. I turned and swung, chopping the hard edge of my right hand into the back and side of his neck. I chopped him all the way down until he lay quietly dozing, his ugly face buried in the thick carpeting.

Then, just as I started to straighten up, it happened. Something moved behind me, and I flung myself sideways to my left, which proved to be fatal. The sap came down squarely on top of my skull. For a moment my eyes seemed to pop from my head, blood gushing out of the empty sockets. I struggled to my feet, groping in a red sea of cold sticky blood, my arms clawing for support. Suddenly, there was another explosion, and my eyes came snapping back into my head as a white blaze of light washed away the blood. Then the walls buckled and the floor undulated and the ceiling came crashing down. I ducked my head and landed face down on the floor, the ceiling crushing me into a cold, inescapable darkness.

13

AWOKE to the sound of running water and the touch of some-thing cold on my forehead. I opened my eyes and stared at the white ceiling, which was where it belonged. I was lying on my bed, and I still had my shoes on. Brittle daggers of pain stabbed at my temples, and I closed my eyes to protect them from the blazing light. The water stopped running and I heard footsteps coming toward the bed. The wet cloth was removed from my forehead, and a colder one took its place. I opened my eyes again and tried to focus on the anxious face of Frank Delaney.

"Hi, buddy," I mumbled, the sound of my voice setting off the pain again.

"How're you feeling, Vince?"

"Great," I said. "Never felt better. How's the wife and kids?"

Frank laughed. "You'll live, I guess. But I wouldn't try to wear a hat for a while."

I should have been angry, but instead I just felt giddy. "Give me a drink," I said, waving my arm toward the night stand and the bottle of bourbon.

Frank got the bottle and we both had a drink. I tried to sit up, but Frank had to help me. That bed felt like it stood at the edge of a precipice, and all I wanted to do was jump off.

"Who slugged me, Frank?"

"I don't know. I found you in that small room, lying there with the rest of the bodies. From the way it looked, you were in better shape than most of them. Lewis was taken to the hospital. Internal injuries, bleeding from the mouth and rectum pretty bad. I don't think he's critical, but damn serious, anyway. The other two creeps left under their own staggering power. They were quite a sight. I felt like holding them and calling in, but I had no idea what had happened, and I didn't want to start something that would get you in trouble. I figured you'd tell me the score, and that would be soon enough to go after those creeps if I had to."

I waved my hand toward the bottle, and he poured me another drink.

"Now, for Christ's sake, don't get stinko."

"Here, have one."

"No. One's all I take on duty."

"You're true blue."

He grinned, his blue eyes warm and friendly. "Give me the goddam bottle," he said, scooping it from the nightstand. "I've never met a drunk yet who didn't want to make everybody else in his own image."

"You're much too good to me," I said, taking the bottle from his hand and pouring myself another one. "Here, have a drink, Frank."

"Go to hell," he said.

"You shouldn't get mad at me. I haven't been well lately."

"Well? You're sick, sick, sick."

"You're so right, right, right. Can I feel my lump?"

"Lumps."

"More than one?"

He nodded, smiling and pointing the neck of the bottle at the top of my head.

"More than two?" I quickly reached up and delicately probed the sensitive area with my finger tips. I had two knots. One dead center, the other a little more to the fore. They were both the size of a pullet egg. That may be a small egg at the supermarket, but on top of your head it ain't small. It's goddam big and painful.

"What's on your mind?" I said.

OVID DEMARIS

"On my mind?" He looked at his watch and winced. "What time did you say this mechanic went home?"

"Five."

"Well, let's go. It's five after five right now."

I jumped off the bed and nearly fell on my face, but Frank reached for me in time. The whole room started to prance and rock. I sat down again. "Give me a second," I said. "I'll be all right."

It was a quarter past five when we reached the garage, but Juan was still there, vacuuming the interior of the Rolls. Frank explained to him why he wanted his fingerprints, and the boy complied without any argument. Then we went out to my car, and Frank dusted the creeper and lifted a dozen good prints.

"I can tell you right now, just from the size, that most of them are not Juan's."

"Things are looking up, finally," I said, handing him the two pieces of friction tape.

Frank examined the ends of the tapes and nodded. "I'll get Ralph in the lab to check them out. Let you know the whole score sometime tomorrow. Is that okay?"

"Fine. Frank, I really appreciate this."

"My pleasure," he said. "Now, how about the mayhem here today? Want to tell me about it?"

"Later," I said. "Right now I'd rather leave things as they are."

"It's your show."

After Frank left, I went back to my room with the idea of napping for a couple of hours. I didn't know where Freddie was, and I didn't much care. He was the sonofabitch who had fingered Marty, and if Marty died I would personally see to it that Freddie got his tail burned, but good. Violence wasn't exactly anything new for Freddie Sharpe. This boy had dished it out plenty of times. Not personally, but his goons had accommodated him in nightclubs all over the country. Freddie would start a fight, and the Killer or the Rock would take over and finish it by breaking the other guy's jaw or cracking his head open. In the retelling of these little episodes in the newspapers, the goons were often forgotten and Freddie came out looking like a wildcat on wheels. That was the way Freddie thought of himself. A real tough guy with a socko right hand. The older he got, the more numerous the fights. Until finally his name had become anathema in night clubs everywhere. When he worked them, the clubs paid him fifty grand a week, otherwise they were scared to see him.

I hung on the edge of sleep a long time, thinking about Freddie and the various members of the claque. I still hadn't met Chauncey, the personal clown. It was strange when you thought of it. Chauncey, the clown who had belonged to the world for so many years, ended up in old age as the personal property of another clown. In my book, Freddie Sharpe was just as big a clown as Chauncey. The only difference between the two men were their bags of tricks. One sang for his dinner, while the other tickled your funny bone. I hadn't been too anxious to speak to Chauncey because, I suppose, I couldn't picture him as a villain. There are people who fit the role, and others who don't, even when they do.

There were two other members, Ray Martin and Al Goldstein, but they were out of town and had been out for at least two weeks. Then, of course, there was Phemie White, who didn't strike me as the type who knew the difference between a gas line and a brake line. That was everybody, I thought, pushing myself more deeply into the soft mattress in search of sleep. Just as I fell asleep, I remembered Loren Mayberry, the personal make-up man, but his image soon got mixed up with that of Phemie. Then I was out cold for nearly five hours.

It was a few minutes after ten when consciousness first stirred. I reached up and felt the top of my head. The swelling had gone down some, but it was still painful, and the headache had persisted. The room was in total darkness, except for the slit of light under the connecting door to Freddie's room. I could hear voices and I sat up, trying to make out words. Then I slipped off the bed and tiptoed to the door, placing my ear against it. When you're a private investigator, listening at keyholes will get you a lot more truth than poetry.

The voice was shrill and feminine. "Freddie, please, now you've got to sit still. How can I work with you moving your head all the time? Now, please, just for Loren. Pretty please."

Freddie, evidently wasn't listening to Loren. "I want Slader out of here in the morning. I don't need him and I don't trust him. Now, you do that for me, Gus."

"But, sweetheart, you don't understand. The bit was a stunt, but what about the press? They don't know that, you know. Not yet, anyway. If you let Slader go, they might get suspicious. Hell, he might even spill it himself. And don't forget—he knows what happened to Marty, and Adela, too. You don't want that getting in the press, do you? Be reasonable, sweetheart—Slader can do us a lot of damage right now."

"Not if I give Nick the word."

"Freddie, you've got to leave Nick alone. He's poison. Let's just pray that Marty doesn't die. God, sweetheart, we'd be in trouble up to our ears. I mean big trouble."

Freddie laughed to dispel the fear. "Marty's in a good private hospital. If he should kick off, which he won't, everything would be taken care of."

"Sure, but what about the death certificate? Those records are available to the police and newsmen."

"So what? The death certificate would be made out in his real name, and there's not a newsman in town who could make the connection. He's just an obscure little pimp. Don't worry about it."

I decided it was time to make my entrance. I turned the knob and gently pushed the door open. Freddie was sitting on a stool before his dressing-table mirror, and Loren Mayberry was carefully massaging his scalp with one of those electric gizmos the barbers use. Freddie was chewing gum and smoking, studying himself in the mirror.

"When murder is involved, there's always something to worry about, Freddie," I said, slowly walking into the room.

Freddie spun around on the stool, pushing Mayberry's hand away. Mayberry stomped his foot and frantically pounded his forehead. Gus Milner tried to paint a smile on his gray face, but the best he could do was twist his lips in a grimace. Freddie aimed that menacing stiff finger at me again.

"How long have you been listening?" he barked, his black eyes cold and deadly. "You're getting too much, man. Too god-dam much. I'm warning you. Don't push me too far."

"That's a two-edged sword," I said. "Don't you push me too far, either. I don't take kindly to being slugged. And, frankly, when I find out who did it, that boy's gonna have a few lumps of his own."

"Now, now, Vince," Gus said, coming forward. "Let bygones be bygones. What's the sense of stirring up more trouble? You got your licks in. Why want more?"

"Gus," I said. "You're a sweet guy, but you're also a goddam big ass-kissing phony. Let me tell you something. In my job, I'm the boss. I'm a free-wheeling, free-dealing operator. I take only the jobs I want, and I handle them in the way I want. Now, this job has been out of control from the start. I figure that's my fault. But from now on things are going to be different. First, Freddie, you better understand that somebody tried to kill you last night. I don't care if Lewis' notes were a stunt or not. Cutting through a brake line is no stunt. My job now is not only protection, but also detection. I'm going to find out who did it, and anybody who gets in my way is liable to get hurt. And you can forget about letting me go. I'm staying to the bitter end. I never quit a job in the middle of it. It's bad for my reputation, and it's bad for my curiosity. The sooner you understand this, the sooner we'll start getting some place."

"Brother," Freddie said. "You take a lot for granted. What makes you think I can't toss you out on your ear if I want to?"

"Don't be stupid," I said. "You've got too many people in the hospital. And, besides, I already have the police working on this case. On the q.t. for now, but that's only as long as I want to keep it that way."

"What do you mean, the police?"

"Fingerprints and other evidence from your garage."

"You're really hot on this murder bit, aren't you?"

"You're damn right. And so should you be. Your life is in the balance, buster."

"What about those fingerprints? How did you get them?"

I explained about the creeper and the pieces of tape. "Does that sound like a stunt to you?"

He shook his head, confused. "I can't believe it. Why should anyone here want to kill me? And besides, it's too much of a coincidence. You know, the notes and then this thing, all at once."

"Maybe it's not a coincidence. Think of it this way. Somebody probably tried to cash in on the other guy's notes."

"I don't follow."

"Well, Lewis said he spread the rumor around. Now, why couldn't somebody get the inspiration from the notes? If someone here really wanted to see you dead, it was a tailor-made opportunity. The police would be trying to check out the notes, trying logically to piece it together from that angle. After all, somebody threatens murder, and it is done. The real murderer, thinking along these lines, would look at this as a foolproof opportunity. You see, the murderer had no way of knowing that it was just a Lewis publicity stunt. All he knew was that your life had been threatened and suddenly a private investigator had been hired. My appearance on the scene forced his hand. You can bet he had been thinking about it for a long while before that."

Freddie still shook his head. "It's unbelievable. I can't buy it. Look, I know everybody around here. There's not a guy here who hates me. Well, maybe there's one or two, but not enough to murder me. Listen, I know these guys. They don't have that kind of guts. Man, it takes real guts to commit murder. Especially a guy like me. That would be a big deal, the cops would go all out."

"But you'd still be dead," I said.

"Okay," he said. "Name your terms. I'm sold."

"First thing. Who slugged me?"

He turned back to the mirror. "I don't know."

"Where were you during the fireworks?"

"In my office with Nick. I told him about Lewis, but I didn't know he was going to do that to him. Nick is an old muscle man. He's a nice guy, but that's the only way he can think."

"How about you, Gus?"

"I don't know, either. I was with Freddie all the time."

"Okay," I said. "I'll find out soon enough."

"Come on, Queenie, shake it up. I've got a date, man," Freddie said to Mayberry.

"Well, I like that," Mayberry squealed. "Freddie, sometimes you're just impossible. I mean really impossible."

"You hate me, Queenie?"

"Now, Freddie, I love you. Don't you know that?"

Freddie grinned, and winked at me in the mirror. "How about sweating a confession out of Queenie? I mean, you know, give him the thumbscrew, the whole rack bit. I'd bet he'd love every minute of it. Right, Queenie?"

Mayberry flushed, turning his face away from me. "That's not fair, Freddie. Not fair at all."

"We're going out on the town tonight, Slader," Freddie said. "You up to it?"

"Yeah, I'm up to it. Who's we?"

"Me, that new pig, Janice Lang, that old pig, Lisa Love, and a buddy of mine, Dirk Dawson, the old American meatball."

Dirk Dawson was another singer, not as big as Freddie, but big enough to pal around with him. He was also on the dramatic end now. All the singers were acting, and all the actors were singing. Every day they were discovering new voices in old actors. Pretty soon even Gary Cooper would be cutting an L.P., no doubt to the accompaniment of galloping hoofs.

"That sounds like real fun," I said.

"Free ride," he said. "Eats and drinks on the house. My house."

I watched Mayberry put the finishing touches to Freddie's make-up. This guy had more things going for him out of jars than most women. The finishing touch was the application of pancake over the chin cut and fading black eye.

"Okay, shamus, let's split."

14

THE ROCK drove us in the Rolls to the Carib, one of the Sunset Strip's most exclusive nightspots. This was my first ride in a Rolls, and it nearly spoiled me for the Ford. The Rock stopped in front, and an ex-admiral opened the door of the car and greeted Freddie most solemnly. "Good evening, Mr. Sharpe."

There was a blue carpet on the sidewalk, and for an answer, Freddie dropped his cigarette on it. The admiral quickly scooped it up without a change of expression.

Another ex-admiral opened the glass door and welcomed us into the exotic splendor of the Carib, which looked like a grandiose set from an old Goerge Raft stinker.

The maître-d' jumped when he saw Freddie come through the door. That beautiful phony smile was enough to make you retch.

"Good evening, Mr. Sharpe. May I escort you to Mr. Dawson's table?"

"Where is it?" Freddie demanded, looking over the room.

"The best table in the house, sir. Stage center."

"Got elbow room around there? Everytime I come here, I've a bunch of creeps sitting on my shoulders."

"Yes, sir. We removed two tables for your convenience."

"Ah, I see the meatball," Freddie said, starting down the steps ahead of the maître-d', who scurried around to his right, trying to get in front of Freddie.

"Relax, buster," Freddie said, stiff-arming him. "I know my way around this joint."

"Yes, sir," he said, bowing his apologies.

I slipped him a five-spot, but he barely looked at me. I figured that was okay. He would need the loot soon for his ulcer.

Dirk Dawson was also Italian, with a head so full of curls that he made Clara Bow look like Yul Brynner. He was so plastered he barely looked up from his glass when we arrived. Freddie slapped him on the back and laughed. The two girls were also riding high. Janice Lang was wearing a low-cut black sheath with shoestring straps that were already beginning to slip. Standing up there, I got a periscope view down her front assembly. Lisa Love had on a strapless, gold-beaded sheath, and I quickly forgot about sweet sixteen and the rose-colored, dewy knockers.

Freddie leaned over and kissed Janice on the neck. First she giggled, then she gave a sharp little cry of surprise. Freddie grinned, wiping his mouth. He had spat down the front of her dress, the glob of spit slowly rolling down into her dark, mysterious valley.

"Mr. Sharpe," she quivered, not knowing whether to smile or cry.

"That's good for you," Freddie said, sitting down between her and Dawson. "Make 'em grow. Listen, from now on you leave them things to me. When I get done with you, Mansfield will look like a member of the D.A.R. Okay?"

She nodded, blinking her lashes. She was having a hard time controlling her emotions. On rare occasion, I feel sorry for the kids lost in this jungle. And this was one of those moments. A year from now, or maybe even less, it will be too late to feel sorry. I never like to waste my sympathy. When you live in a big city and get around a bit, you've got to conserve it. There's never enough to go around.

I sat down between Janice and Lisa. "You look disgustingly sober," Lisa said. "I hate sober men, especially in night clubs."

"Sorry," I said. "I'll do my best to catch up."

There were three or four buckets of champagne around the table, and Lisa handed me one. "All right," she said. "Get started, partner."

"Who's that?" Dawson drawled in a thick, slurred voice.

"That's my shamus," Freddie said. "He's gonna see that nobody murders me."

"Ah, screw that," Dawson said. "What's wrong with murder?"

"Nothing," Freddie said. "As long as I'm not the corpse."

"Ah, go on. You'd make a fine corpse. Beautiful corpse. We'd put you in the Pantages and charge admission. Man, you'd be great. Take my word for it. You'd break all records."

I had three quick glasses of champagne. If you've got to listen to that type of garbage, it's a good thing to deaden the senses first. Freddie wasn't losing any time with the champagne, either. Waiters floated in on tiptoe, replacing dead soldiers, and floated out again without making a sound. At twelve o'clock, the lights dimmed, and some fat dame in a white satin dress came out and started to sing.

I couldn't place the face and body, but I knew the voice. It was Julie Walker, and she had been one of the greatest kid stars of her time. Now twenty years, six marriages and four nervous breakdowns later, there was only a voice left, a voice screeching in the wilderness.

A glaze had settled over Freddie's eyes, and his movements had become slow and deliberate. He had a peculiar little smile at the corner of his mouth as he watched Julie Walker.

"Pig," he said, turning his attention back to the table. "Know what's wrong with that pig, shamus?"

"No," I said. "And I'm not too greatly interested."

"Well, I'll tell you anyway. Now you listen, Janice, baby. This is gonna be educational." He turned his head and waved to Julie. She looked straight out over his head.

"I'll tell you," he said. "She's only got one tit. I mean it. Ain't that a gas, man?"

"You're silly," Janice said. "I can plainly see she has two."

Freddie shook his head angrily. "Naw, naw, naw. She's got only one, I tell you. I know. She's got two bubbies, but only one tit. Get it?" He laughed, dropping his arm around Janice's bare shoulder, his fingers playing with the slipping strap. "How many tits do you have, baby?"

"Two, silly," she said, trying to keep it light.

"Yeah. Prove it. Let's see 'em. Come on now. Show us. Want me to help you?" His fingers reached down, and she caught his hand.

"Don't, please. Not here."

"Ah, screw them. Who cares? Come on, show me."

"Come on, Freddie, finish the story," I said, trying to side-track his attention.

"What story?"

"Julie," I said. "Girl with one tit."

"Oh, yeah," he said, rubbing his hand against his forehead. It looked wet and clammy. "Some guy got so hot one night he just bit it off. That's why she's so nutty."

"That's awful," Janice said. "That's mean."

Lisa Love laughed for the first time that evening. All she had done so far was drink. For a while I felt her knee pressing against my leg, but when I didn't return the pressure she pulled it away. After that she concentrated all her attention on getting drunk.

"You know who bit it off?" Lisa said, staring drunkenly at me.

"I haven't the faintest idea," I said.

"I'll tell you," Freddie said. "Her daddy did it."

"Her stepfather," Lisa said.

"What's the difference?" Dawson said, coming out of his alcoholic haze for a moment.

"There's a big difference," Lisa said.

"Yeah," Freddie said. "There are more stepdaddies. Man, everybody in this town has been a stepdaddy at least three times."

"She was only fifteen," Lisa said. "Made a deep traumatic impression on her. She's been to analysts for years. Didn't do any good. She's been a lush and hype. She's had it all. Nothing helps."

Freddie raised his hands to silence the table. "Did anybody here ever see it?" He waited for emphasis. "It's a riot," he said. "A real gas."

When Julie Walker left the stage, we ordered dinner. Everybody had steak except Dawson, who had spaghetti and meat balls.

That steak tasted real good, and found plenty of room in my empty stomach. To watch Dawson eat was an experience I could have done without. He leaned over his plate and shoveled the stuff in with two forks, splattering tomato sauce in all directions. When he got done, his face looked like he had measles.

After dinner I stuck to coffee. The waiter finally left a pot of it in front of me. Throughout the dinner I had noticed Dawson staring at one of the waiters. Finally he grabbed the waiter's sleeve and pulled his face down to his.

"How'd you do it?" he demanded, a puzzled expression on his face.

"Do what, sir?"

"Come on, now. Don't play with me. How'd you do it? I want to know, goddammit."

"I'm sorry, sir, I don't know what you mean."

"You do, too." And he gave a yank on the sleeve, pulling the waiter against the table. The waiter's face clouded, but he didn't fight back.

"I'm sorry, sir. But I have to clear this table."

Dawson leaned back in his chair, still holding on to the sleeve. "I saw you there. I know it was you. How did you get out of that tank?"

By this time even my interest had quickened. Freddie had the two girls had stopped talking and were watching Dawson.

"What tank, sir?"

"You know what tank. The tank at Belsen. The one where they were supposed to gas you. I saw you there. Don't tell me you weren't there. I saw you just yesterday."

Freddie turned and stared at me. "This cat's flipped, dad."

Dawson turned to glare at Freddie and lost the waiter. "Come back here," he yelled at the fleeing waiter.

Freddie shrugged his shoulders and stood up. "Come on, let's blow this joint. Man, you've had it."

Dawson reached out and pulled Freddie back down in the chair. "Listen, you don't understand. I saw this guy getting it in a gas chamber just yesterday."

"Sure, sure," Freddie said.

"For Christ's sake, don't humor me," Dawson said. "I tell you I saw this Jew in a Belsen gas chamber just yesterday. It was at Lorain's house. She got one of those Nazi's films. Man, you never saw anything like it. God, the drama, the suspense—it was too much."

"Yeah," Freddie said. "Tell us about it. Sounds like a gas." He laughed, slapping Janice across the shoulders. "Did you get it?" he cried. "A gas in the gas chamber. Man, I'm wild tonight."

"The film was stolen by some of our boys during the invasion. Man, those Nazis were incredible. They actually took films of the executions. Imagine this if you can. A hundred Jews herded inside a small concrete chamber. All naked. Men and women and even children. They're all gonna die. You know this from the beginning. And they know it, too. Some are bawling, some are praying and some, man, are doing other things, if you know what I mean. To watch those faces, when the gas starts coming into the chamber is fantastic. I'm telling you, it's the wildest experience. Those Nazis shot the scene from all angles. Long shots, medium shots, close-ups. They were using a half dozen cameras. They were shooting from all angles. Low, medium, high, and one camera was even in the ceiling, shooting down with a wide-angle lens. I've seen a lot of this kind of stuff, but man this was the wildest. The suspense was unbearable. You knew they were all going to get it, but it didn't make any difference. You were still on the edge of your seat."

"The edge you're on, fella, has nothing to do with a seat," I said, standing up. "Come on Freddie, it's time to say by-by to the sick man."

Freddie didn't argue. I guess he had had enough, too. It takes all kinds to make a world, I'm told. But this kind we can do without.

"Now, wait," Dawson said. "This gets better all the time. I've just started." The excitement had sobered him up considerably. "This actually happened. Don't you understand? It's photographic history."

Lisa stood up and placed a hand on my sleeve. She was pale and shaken. I put my arm around her waist, supporting her. "I think I'm going to be ill," she said. "Please walk me to the powder room."

"Wait for me," Janice called, hurrying after us.

I deposited them at the entrance, where a uniformed maid took over. Back at the table, Dawson and Freddie were arguing. I let them go at it without listening. I was tired. I'd had it for the day. Give me a good old-fashioned murder with good old-fashioned people any time. You can keep these jaded perverts.

Lisa went home in a cab, and Dawson went across the street to another joint. I sat in front with the Rock in the Rolls, and Freddie and Janice sat in back. There was a lot of whispering and rustling of material. Now and then I could hear a harsh, frightened "no," but the struggle continued. At the Hilltop, Freddie jumped out and Janice refused to leave the car. I got out and stood beside him. The Rock stayed behind the wheel.

"Come on," Freddie said. "Stop the coy bit. I've got something I want to show you."

"No," she said. "I want to go home. I'm tired. Please, Mr. Sharpe, let me go home."

"Mr. Sharpe? I told you to call me Freddie. You have all night. Come on, don't be cute. Let's go."

"I can't," she said. "I'm ill."

"What?"

"I can't, really."

"You want that part in *Run for Home?* Do you?"

"Yes, but I can't. Not tonight. Maybe next week. I promise."

"Yeah. Well, either you come in tonight, or don't bother reporting for work. You're out and I'll personally see to it that you stay out. I've got influence in this town, kid. Be smart."

She stared at him a long time, then quietly stepped out of the car and followed him into the house, down the long empty hallway and into his bedroom. The last thing I heard was the scraping of the key in the lock.

15

SLEPT forever. And the dreams I had were not printable. It was one of those horrible nights that never seem to end. You go from one bad dream to another without a blank spot anywhere. And each dream gets worse than the previous one. I suppose a Freudian analyst could have connected it with the events of that day and night, but that wouldn't have helped very much. I'd still have preferred to forget the whole thing.

The last dream did it. I gave a wild start and sat straight up in bed. The drapes were drawn and the blackness was like a weight pressing against me. I didn't know if it was morning, noon or night. I slid out of bed and yanked the drapes open. The blast of sunlight nearly blinded me. I staggered back to the bed and closed my eyes, folding my arm over my face. Slowly, I opened my eyes again, gradually adjusting to the light. My head still ached like a bad tooth. I peered at my watch. It was ten minutes after two. I staggered into the bathroom and shower. Good champagne has recuperative powers. Especially if you try to move too quickly the next morning. You've got to take it slow and easy so you don't stir the sediment waiting like a bomb in your stomach. The cold water pulled the fuse for me. After that I was fine. I shaved and dressed, this time wearing a jacket so I could have the rod where it belonged, at my side. I was all done taking bumps the hard way in this house. I tried the connecting door but it was still locked. Before going out to the dining room, I drifted into the lobby to see who I could find for a little chat. The first one I saw was Chauncey.

I was still in awe of this wonderful man. At least, that's what he had been to me many years ago. I hoped he hadn't changed too much. He was talking to Tiny Tim, and I waited until he had finished.

"Chauncey," I said. "I'm Vince Slader."

"Oh, yes," he said. "I want to shake your hand, sir. That was a mighty fine display of courage yesterday. Happy to make your acquaintance." He held out his hand and I took it, realizing that it wasn't much larger than a girl's. He had very tiny hands and feet. In fact, all of his features were small. Eyes, nose, ears, mouth. And yet he was an average-sized man.

"Will you join me for breakfast or lunch? I haven't eaten yet, and I would very much appreciate your company."

"Be honored to, sir. Have you met Mr. Crosby?"

Tiny Tim waved, and I nodded. "Yes, I've had the pleasure."

"Well, sir, lead on."

On my way up the long hallway to the dining hall, I remembered I hadn't noticed whether the living room was crowded. You quickly get used to that sort of thing. For all I knew it could have been filled with a delegation of Eskimo nudists.

Chauncey ordered a hamburger and malt, while I ordered a dozen pancakes and half a dozen eggs. I was mildly hungry.

"A big man should eat big," Chauncey said.

"Yes, that's what I've always said."

He grinned. "I don't know a thing about you, Mr. Slader, but I like your type. Every man I've ever met that looked like you was sincere and straightforward. I realize that this doesn't sound very scientific, but you know something? I don't care. I think a man should trust his own instinct. Should depend on his judgment, whether it makes sense to others or not. That's my philosophy, Mr. Slader. I believe in the integrity and judgment of men. I don't care who they are. A man with enough years of living should know something about life and people. You don't need a college diploma to tell you it's raining out. And you don't need one to tell you if your stomach hurts. Well, then, why should you need one to tell you how to live your life? I've had a good life, Mr. Slader. Very good." He stopped and studied my features a long time. "Good up to a point, sir."

"Please go on," I said. "I'm fascinated."

"Thank you, sir. If I can fascinate a man of your quality, then I haven't completely failed. You see, sir, I was just about to say that I had a good life—up to a point. The point, sir, is that I've outlived my talent and, therefore, my usefulness. That's a very sad dilemma. All the philosophers have not been able to solve this riddle. It is a riddle created by the refinement of our civilization. Too much emphasis on life per se, and not enough on its quality. I've always believed in quality, and very little in quantity. It's not the years that make a life worthwhile. A person can live a full life in a few short years, while another can waste a century."

I smiled, very pleased with myself. I looked at him, at his marvelously expressive face and suddenly I felt grateful. He hadn't disappointed me. He was a court jester, a worn-out clown, but he still had integrity and stature.

"Don't take me wrong," he said. "I'm not knocking education. I think it's great when it's used correctly. All I'm trying to say is that it's not the great panacea it's cracked up to be. Too many educated men are unhappy. And that goes for riches and success, too."

"Well," I said. "What is the answer?"

"The answer?" He scratched his head and gave me that famous gloomy smile. "I only wish I knew. What a contribution that would be to the world! Oh, believe me, I've thought about it. One time I even tried to put it down on paper. But suddenly, in the middle of the book, I lost it. It just slipped away. All I had left were words. Thousands of silly, sad, empty words. Smarter men than me have tried to crystallize this thought and failed just as badly. All they left us with were words like truth and beauty. Oh, they had long lengthy discussions about them. They tried to explain them, and the harder they tried the faster the idea slipped away. It's all very sad."

"How about love and religion?"

"The same thing," he said, shaking his head. "Breed twice as much misery as happiness. Sometimes when I really think, like at night, you know, when I'm all alone in my room and everything is quiet, it comes to me. And I hold on to it for an instant. Then poof. It's gone."

"Don't quit," I said. "Keep trying. It's the only way. And, if you ever find that answer, I want to know about it."

"You will." He stopped and grinned at me foolishly. "Look at me," he said, "monopolizing the whole conversation. That's a true sign of old age. Senility. That's what they call it today. Sir, I hate that word. It's sordid and degrading. It has a nasty connotation. Please, excuse me for lecturing you."

"No excuse necessary," I said. "I've enjoyed it very much."

"Now, sir, did you want to ask me anything?"

"No," I said. "I just wanted the pleasure of your company. I admired you very much when I was a kid."

"Admiration is good for children," he said. "I'm not so sure about adults."

Just then Carlton Stone stepped up to the table and sat down.

"Am I breaking in on anything?" He had a smug smile on his face, made even more smug by the pipe clenched between his teeth.

Chauncey immediately got to his feet, bringing his hand up in a perky little salute.

"See you around, Mr. Slader."

I stood up and we shook hands. "I hope so," I said. "It's been a pleasure."

Stone waited until Chauncey had left the dining room before turning up his nose. "Pompous little jerk," he said.

"Did you ever take a close look at yourself with that book-of-the-month pipe stuck in your face?"

Color flooded up his neck, but he smiled like he didn't give a damn.

"Well, at least, I have a sense of humor."

"I'll bet."

"Okay, okay, I apologize. It was a stinking thing to say. Chauncey's all right. It's just the paradox that bugs me. Talks like a saint and acts like a jackass. You ought to see him in action when Freddie snaps his fingers. It's sickening."

"Maybe," I said. "But that man has more character in his little finger than you have in your whole spinal column. His body is for hire, but not his mind or spirit. What's worse? Doing a few pratfalls or writing garbage?"

That brought him up in his chair. "I give up," he said, laughing, but there was a peculiar little quaver in his voice. "Let's start all over again."

"What's there to start?"

"Oh, please, desist. I surrender. I lie prostrate at your feet."

That word *prostrate* was a good one. It put the whole household in a nutshell. "Tell me something," I said, "now that we're fast friends. Who slugged me?"

"You don't know?" He pondered that question without my assistance a moment. "Maybe it's better if you don't. You were real great, by the way. I saw the whole thing. Man, you do the kind of things I write about. What a wallop. Don't ever get mad at me, please—I haven't been well lately."

"Stop stalling," I said.

"Look, you don't want me to get slugged, too, do you? Don't answer that."

"You won't get slugged. This is strictly between the two of us."

He bit on the pipe stem, grinding his teeth into it, while he studied my face. "The Rock did it with a blackjack."

I ordered more coffee and told myself to keep calm. There was a time for everything, and this wasn't it.

"What a head you've got. Just one of those blows would have killed me. You should have heard the sound. It sounded like a club beating against a pumpkin."

"Thanks a lot."

"No, no, no. I mean it was that loud." He felt the top of his head, grimacing. "Really, I thought you were dead. Violence is a peculiar thing. You read about it and see it in the movies and television, but, man—when you see the real thing in action it's a lot different. Scares the hell out of you. I had the shakes for an hour afterwards. Damn near messed my pants on the spot. I'm not kidding. That really gripped me. Wow!"

"I know," I said. "It's actually worse watching than doing. You don't have time to think about it when you're involved."

"I'd still rather watch."

"What kind of writing do you do?"

"Odds and ends. Mostly odds."

"Write scripts?"

"I'm a doctor," he said. "A dialogue doctor. I polish up Freddie's line. Make sure they don't mess up his personality. You see, Freddie must be Freddie no matter what the role. If he played Peter the Great, it would be old Peter who changed, not Freddie. Even song lyrics are changed to fit Freddie's personal charm. I insert such touching words as cat, dig, flip, gas, kook; all ring-a-ding-ding stuff."

I shook my head and stood up. "It was fun," I said. "And educational. See you around, Stone."

"Sure," he said, his chubby face turned up to me. Suddenly his eyes shot past my head, and he quickly motioned for me to look around. "See the tray the waiter is carrying out?"

I turned too late and only caught the back of the disappearing waiter. "What about it?"

"Shredded wheat, strawberries and champagne. That's the giveaway, man. Freddie's shacked up with some chick. His favorite diet when he's making it like Flynn. One time he never left the room for a solid week. You should have seen the chick. Man, she came out on her knees. Not Freddie. He had someone else that same night. That man is incredible. At first I envied him."

"And now?"

"No more, man. He's sick. I'm glad I'm normal."

I grinned and started to walk out.

"Hey, Slader. Listen—someday, when I write that great American epic, I'll send you a personally inscribed copy."

"Do that," I said.

"I will," he said, and there was a brittle note of desperation in his voice. "You'll see. I mean it."

Freddie grumbled angrily when I knocked on the door. I walked away, feeling guilty. I wanted to help that kid in there, but what good would it have done? She was making her first offering to that ugly God called success. Some people will pay more than others for what they want. Maybe that's why they usually get it. However, what may seem big to one person may be quite small to another. Who's to know? The right kind of help at the wrong time can bring more destruction than good.

I stretched out on the bed, determined to mind my own business. The way things were developing, it would be enough to keep me busy. I was positive that the attempted murder had been tried by a member of the claque. I had met and talked to most of the candidates without any tangible result. Somewhere in the back of my mind an impression was forming, but so far I had nothing concrete. I wasn't any farther ahead than I had been Friday afternoon in Goldman's office. Usually the most important element a cop or private investigator looks for in such cases is motivation. Except for psychopaths, murderers most always have pretty good reasons urging them on. I would place money as number one on that list. Then love and hate in that order. In this case, I could forget about money and love. Everybody was overpaid, with nothing to gain by killing the Golden Goose. And as far as love was concerned, it was just a dirty word. That left me with hate.

Now there was a popular emotion. The whole place seethed with it. It was the energy that kept all the little broken wheels turning at a full clip. All I had to do was find the little broken wheel that turned the fastest. And that wasn't going to be easy.

I was convinced of one thing. Whoever had cut that brake line had gotten the idea from the threatening notes. Somebody with sufficient hate had jumped on Lewis's bandwagon. Lewis, in my mind, had been eliminated from that possibility. Otherwise, he never would have released the story to the papers. So who did that leave? Just about an even dozen.

Just then the telephone kindly interrupted.

"Slader," I said, stretching out on the bed again.

"You sound sleepy," Frank said. "Been taking it easy, eh? Boy, I wish I had your job. What a soft touch."

"Keep it up," I said. "You're telling it."

"Good news, Vince. Real good."

I felt a tightening in my stomach. "Yeah?"

"I got a fine set of prints, and they weren't Juan's either."

"Who?"

"Take it easy. I don't know who yet. I air-mailed them to Washington. Should hear in a couple days."

"Air mail?"

"Vince, my hands were tied. I couldn't wirephoto without explaining. And I didn't think you'd want that."

"Well, dammit, what's that good news you greeted me with?"

"The prints will work out. Don't worry. And the tapes matched like your mother's eyes. Perfect. No doubt about it. Isn't that good news?"

I felt silly. "Sorry, Frank. I guess this case has me reeling. It's fine news. It positively confirms something I already suspected. The job was done right here in the garage by somebody in the claque. I'll keep my fingers crossed on the prints. I've been known to hit a little luck now and then. Who knows?"

"Leaving tomorrow?"

"Yeah. At ten in the morning. I'll wire you my address as soon as I get there."

"Fine. Have a nice trip, and don't do anything I wouldn't do."

"I already have," I said.

"You're awful, that's all I can say."

"Does Helen want a personally autographed picture of Freddie? Be glad to send her one."

"Drop dead," Frank said.

"Let the little woman live. What's the matter with you?"

"That's living?"

"Sure. This is America's number-one passion."

"Good-by, Vince. Have a nice trip."

"Wait. How about the size of the prints? Could they tell anything from that?"

"Some. They're unusually large. But you know. Some little guys have big fingers and vice versa. Hard telling."

"Thanks, Frank. I truly appreciate this."

"See you," he said.

The rest of the day dragged into evening while I drank bourbon and listened to the radio. I felt good about the big fat set of prints. It was my first solid clue. There was a chance, of course, that the prints belonged to an innocent party, but that chance was greatly reduced by the matching of the pieces of friction tape. In such instances, it's better to assume a person guilty until proven otherwise.

I had dinner around nine-thirty and wandered into the living room in search of incriminating fingers. The place was deserted except for the redhead of the night before. She lay on the same sofa, in the same position, except this time it was left thigh that was revealed for my lecherous admiration.

I stopped before the sofa and gazed down at her, first at the white, soft thigh, then the voluptuous hips, up past the flat tummy to the fat breasts, the smooth throat, the full carmine lips, coming to rest on the brown flecked eyes of the genuine redhead.

"I'm Slader," I said.

"I know," she said.

"That give you an edge."

"I'm Carolyn Montrose."

"It sounds like music," I said. "Your parents were imaginative."

She giggled, and it was straight out of Brooklyn. "It's my agent's idea, silly."

"Oh," I said, trying to show intense disappointment.

"You really think it's musical?"

"It swings."

"Gee, thanks."

I looked at her some more, including the thigh. "I'm bored," I said, striving for dimension.

"Oh, me too. This place is getting to be an awful drag."

"Maybe we can do something about that."

"You think so?"

"Sure. How about joining me for a drink?" I paused for emphasis. "In my room."

"Gee, I don't drink. It's bad for your complexion."

"Really? I hadn't noticed lately. I'll have to take a closer look when I shave tomorrow."

"Not you, silly."

I had made the pitch; now it was up to her. "Well," I said. "I think I'll go have that drink. Nice meeting you. Hope to see you around again."

I took one step and her voice stopped me. "I don't drink," she said. "But I'll go with you if you want to talk."

"I love to talk," I said. "It's my favorite indoor sport."

She pulled her legs around, revealing both thighs. My enthusiasm mounted. She stood up, pulling at her dress, that bustline even bigger than I had suspected.

"This way," I said, taking her arm.

"I know," she said. "You're next to Freddie. Gee, I sure think he's nice. Don't you? I just die when he sings. He's got the prettiest mouth. Did you ever notice it? Would you believe he's thirty-seven? He certainly doesn't look it. He doesn't look any more than thirty. I've known lots of men thirty who looked older than Freddie. I'll bet he'll look good when he's sixty. You know, like Cary Grant and Gary Cooper. Or like Bing Crosby. I met him once. Gee, he's a wonderful man. You'd think because he's so rich and famous he'd be stuck-up and dull. But he's not. Not one bit. Oh, I just love that man."

By this time we were in the room and I was pouring myself a drink. I had escorted her to the bed, carefully maneuvering her past the easy chair. She bounced on the bed, her hands clasped in her lap. I sat next to her, sliding my arm around her waist.

"Yeah," I said. "Bing always struck me as a regular *guy*."

"Oh, he is. Gee!" And she exhaled loudly. "There are a lot of wonderful people in this business. That's why I'm so anxious to get my break. I want to be a part of all this. It's so glamorous. Don't you think so?"

"Immensely." I brought my hand under her breast, appalled by the sheer weight of it.

"Now, take my agent. He says I've got all the major quali- ties. And he knows, too. He's handled some big people. Some of the biggest names in the business. He's a wonderful man. You should hear him talk to producers. He knows them all by their first names. And they listen to him, too. He's not afraid to tell them what he thinks. And they respect him for his courage."

By now I had explored both breasts in detail. It was time to work the zipper.

"I've done two small parts so far. And I just loved every min- ute of it. Gee, it was exciting. Did you ever go on a set, you know, in a sound stage to see a movie being shot?"

"No," I said. "I've missed that. I'll bet it's great, though."

The zipper came down to the tip of her spine, and I carefully reached across her shoulders and started pulling down the dress.

All this time she was talking, lowering her arms to accommodate me in my task.

"Oh, it sure is great. You have no idea unless you actually see it. You can just feel the excitement when the director says: 'roll 'em.'"

I twisted the snaps and the elastic nearly tore my finger off. It was that eager for release. The bra hung loosely on the tips of her breasts. All I had to do was touch it and it fell into her lap. She picked it up, examined it casually before placing it on the bed near her, then continued her monologue.

"As I said, I had two minor parts, but they were in major productions. And that makes a big difference, you know. My agent says it's better to get a walk-on in a major production than a leading role in a B stinker. Don't you think he's right?"

"Sure, the guy is a hundred per cent correct. Why don't you lie down and relax?"

She looked down at her partially nude body and leaned back on the bed. I smiled at her, nodding my agreement to what she was saying, and gently pulled the dress across her hips, collecting her panties along the way. She raised her hips at the right moment and everything went off as smooth as the launching of a submarine.

"You know, I'd like for you to meet my agent. He's really a sweet guy. He's a real good friend of Freddie. That's why Freddie invited me up here. I've been coming over here for three weeks now. It's been loads of fun. Be careful, now, your beard is scratching me. Remember, they're very tender. Freddie didn't hardly say a word to me the first week I was here. I guess he had forgotten who I was. Not that he should remember little me. After all, we were just introduced once. But lately he's been talking to me. Asked me what I thought about his house the other day, and we stood and talked for almost five minutes."

"That must have been a great thrill," I said, lifting my head to look at her.

"Oh, it was. Ooooh, he just sends me, if you know what I mean."

"No. But I wish I did right now."

"I saw him in Vegas last year, and I nearly died. He comes out on the stage and just sings, his hands and head moving with the beat. Gosh, I better stop talking about it, it just gets me all excited."

"I'm glad something does," I said, sitting up. "I think I'll have another drink and call it a day."

"You mad or something?"

"Me?"

"Well, the way you just got up and all."

"Don't be foolish. I always pause for refreshment. I wish I had some Coca Cola."

"Why don't you get some? I'd like a Coke right now. I'm awfully thirsty."

"Well, let me ring a ding-ding right now," I said, phoning the dining room.

"Gee, Freddie says that all the time."

"That's true. Know what they say about great minds?"

"You're funny, you know it?"

"I hope not as funny as I look right now."

"No, I don't mean that. I mean you're nice funny. You're very nice to talk to. It's not often I find someone I can talk to. Most men only want one thing. It's really disgusting if you know what I mean."

"All too well."

"Just because I'm stacked like you know what, they think they can just do anything they want. It's annoying. Sometimes it's much more fun just to talk."

"Did you ever think of combining the two?"

"I don't understand what you mean. I knew one guy in Miami who couldn't even wait to get you in his room. He tried it everywhere, in the hallway or storefront, standing up and all. He was real disgusting. I hated him. If he hadn't been a producer and a friend of my agent, I wouldn't even have talked to him. Gee, I just can't stand people like that. You know, they're like animals, or something. I was glad when his wife arrived."

"Meet anybody interesting in Havana?"

She raised her head, surprised by the question. "How did you know I was in Havana? Gee, you must be a mind reader or something."

"Not really. It's quite obvious that you're a well-traveled young lady. Hollywood, Vegas, Miami, Havana, all the places with the plush hotels, the big swimming pools and the money crowd. I think I saw you in a few of those places."

"Did you ever see so many girls? I never could understand that. Most of them don't even work. You know, they're not models or actresses or anything. I guess some of them are whores."

"I wouldn't be surprised."

There was a knock at the door and I opened it slightly, just wide enough for the Filipino boy to slip the bottle through.

"Here, have a drink. Wouldn't want you to get laryngitis."

"Thanks. You're real nice. I like you. In a way, you're a lot like my agent. He always says funny things. Things sometimes I don't understand. But I don't mind as long as they're not mean things. I usually can tell if it's mean by the tone of the voice. His voice kind of changes, and the look in his eyes, too." She was sitting up, drinking from the bottle, her full red lips curved around the neck of the bottle, her nude body reflecting the pink glow of the lamp. It was a ripe, seductive body, overdeveloped in some areas, but very young and very firm. I walked over and gently pushed her down, taking the Coke bottle from her hand.

"Lie down," I said. "I want to talk to you for a change."

I said the usual things one says at such times and she listened as long as I had my mouth on top of hers. It kept me busy there for a few frantic moments. Afterwards, I let her talk to her heart's content. I haven't slept that soundly in years.

16

CAROLYN MONTROSE was gone when I awoke the next morning. It was a few minutes after eight, and I felt strong and rested. I had probably gotten a good nine hours of sound, solid sleep, the kind that penetrates right to the bones. It was one of those clear, brilliant mornings that make you glad to be alive without a reason. Everything else equal, weather often works as a barometer on my psyche. I even sang a couple of choruses of *Vesti la Giubba* from *Pagliacci*. It was apropos. Laugh, clown, laugh. The case may be snafued, but the sun is shining and you had a spirited tussle the night before.

I packed my bags and left them to be taken to the plane with the rest of the baggage. The dining room was crowded, and I sat down with Tiny Tim and Phemie White. This was my first personal contact with Auntie Mame and I expected a lot more than I received. She barely acknowledged my presence when Tiny Tim did the honors. The mile-long silver and onyx cigarette holder fluttered aridly into space, depositing ashes all over the table, including my coffee. Her outfit was beyond the powers of description. You had to be there, as they say. And *there* was in the midst of the roaring twenties, with the flat-chested, long-waisted velvet sack, ropes of pearls measured to bang against the navel, cloche hat, bobbed hair, beaded bag and, so help me, a feather boa.

"How long have you been with Freddie?" I posed as an ice breaker, noticing her thin slender hands and long delicately tapered fingers.

"Darling, I never count years. Only money."

I chewed on that awhile, letting my eyes wander around the room. Except for Freddie and Janice, the claque was present en masse. Gus caught my eye and waved. His gray face looked almost relaxed. Freddie's shacking up was good for Gus.

I returned my attention to the table and addressed another question at Mame.

"I understand you went to Palm Springs yesterday."

She fixed me with an icy stare and a voice to match.

"Darling, you're much too nosy."

"Curious," I corrected. "Just wondered how Adela was coming along."

"Adela is not coming along, if you must know. Now, will you let me finish my breakfast without the obnoxious sound of your vapid voice? If you must ask these questions, I suggest you choose a more suitable place and time. I don't appreciate interrogation with my breakfast."

She didn't wait for an answer but stood straight up, all ten feet of her, and clattered away on her high heels. I was acquainted with the antipathy of the Lesbian for the male, but this dame had a sharper tongue than most of them.

Tiny Tim waited before giving full vent to his giggle. "Man, she's a kick, eh? She's got it in for men. The bigger they are, the more she hates them. I get along fine with her. I don't present any threat to her masculinity."

"Yeah, well, she presents one to mine."

He giggled again. "That question you asked her about how long she's been here. Four years. Was a Broadway actress for ages, then she ran a dramatic school here in Hollywood before coming to Freddie."

"How do they get along?"

"Fine. She hates his guts, and he doesn't even know she exists."

Milner joined us at this point, and Tiny Tim left. "Beautiful day for a plane ride," he said, sitting down in Mame's vacated chair.

"I'm surprised," I said. "I didn't know you noticed weather in Hollywood, with so many other more important things to keep you occupied."

"Vince, we're human, too. Incidentally, what did the female impersonator have to say?"

"Oh, she just slammed my big foot right down my throat."

"She's a dog," he said. "This bit about Adela has hit her hard. I talked with the doc in Palm Springs last night, and from what he told me her visit there was a panic. Seeing Adela like that really broke her up. They had to give her a sedative. I guess she's in love with the kid."

"Does she know Freddie was involved?"

"Not from us. But the kid no doubt told her."

"It's too bad," I said. "Too bad about Adela and too bad about Phemie."

"Yeah, I guess so. I suppose she can't help how she feels. If she wasn't such a bitch all the time, it wouldn't be so bad. Nobody can talk to her. She knows it all."

"How about Freddie?"

"Well, you know Freddie. He always stays in control. If he can't, out they go. She knows better than to antagonize Freddie."

I finished my coffee, and the conversation turned to such aimless subjects as the sales of records, the price of a good pair of English boots and how it's impossible for anyone to really win big money in Vegas.

The ride to the airport was made in complete silence. I sat in the front of the Rolls with the Rock, and the Killer drove. Gus sat in the back with Freddie and Janice. She held Freddie's hand all the way and he never once opened his eyes. It was a tender scene. The Killer, I had learned, was not coming to Kansas with us. This, I told myself, was the real reason for his fierce, sullen expression. He had glanced at me when I first reached the car, and the raw hatred in those black eyes had stopped me cold. I was thankful for the precious little equalizer pressing so affectionately at my left side. It was such a warm and comforting assurance of invincibility.

We arrived half an hour late, but no one seemed too excited about it. I guess they were used to Freddie. The Killer drove the Rolls onto the ramp, right up to the plane. Harry Goldman was there to meet us, surrounded by his own entourage of stooges. They were waiting by the aluminum ladder, beneath the oval opening in the fat silver belly.

A gray-haired man with an Ivy League crew cut gingerly stepped up and opened the rear door, offering Freddie his best public-relations smile.

"Mr. Goldman is awaiting you, Mr. Sharpe."

Freddie opened his eyes and bounced out of the car. "Where's my gang?" he called.

"They're all inside, sir."

"H.G., you old fart," Freddie yelled, as Goldman rushed over to embrace him.

"Freddie, darling, I've come all the way over here just to bid you a *bon voyage*."

"It better be," Freddie backed away, his eyes narrowing. "I'm in no mood for a lecture."

"Lecture! Lecture, smecture. This is your father talking to you, dear boy. This advice I would give only to my first son. It comes from the heart." And he slapped his chest like a gorilla sighting a mate. "I know you, darling, and I love you. It is only natural and good that I would want to help you. You are part of my great big family of lovely children, and I love to help them all. Freddie, darling, your welfare comes first with me. You are the prize, the jackpot in the crackerjack box, you are Goldman Studios. Wherever you go, your name is linked with mine. Can you wonder why my heart bleeds for you, dear boy, when I think of all the silly, prankish things you do? You are not only jeopardizing this great talent the Good Lord has bestowed on your fair head, but you are also dragging the wonderful name of Goldman through the mud and filth of a million minds. The Goldman name has stood for honor and dignity among all sorts of men. It is a name with a tradition, with a family tree longer than the Kings and Queens of England. Don't soil that name, darling. It is a name worthy of respect."

His pink chins jiggled and his blue nose sniffed indignantly as he spoke. Freddie stood with his hands on his hips, shaking his head first in annoyance, then in gradual amusement.

"H.G., you're too much, man."

Goldman shook a handful of fat stubby fingers in front of Freddie's face. He cleared his throat with a short harsh cough. "Darling, I know what's going on in your mind, and I don't like it. You're an ungrateful boy. You keep me awake night after night, worrying and wondering what pile of crap you're standing in. Oh, Freddie, my sweet boy, don't break my heart. Be a good boy, please, darling, for me. For good old H.G. who loves you like a first-born son. Go to Kansas and do the picture, dear boy, without any monkey busi—"

At that moment, there was a loud whoop from inside the plane. Goldman's head snapped around, his mouth opened, his lips still shaped to form the unfinished word.

Dirk Dawson came stumbling out of the plane, stopping on the aluminum ladder, clutching a bottle in one hand and supporting himself with the other. His face was dirty, his hair tangled and matted, and he hadn't shaved since I had last seen him on Saturday night.

"Dad … I … am … here," he called, reeling with laughter. "The admiral reporting to the general." He executed a salute, touching his forehead with the neck of the bottle. Suddenly he held the bottle up, letting the whisky splash on top of his head.

Freddie doubled over, holding his stomach, howling with laughter. "Hey, dad, crazy." Freddie ran up the steps, and, as the two singers embraced, Freddie drank from Dawson's bottle held up above his head.

"How about a little hair oil, dad?" Dawson laughed, pulling the bottle from Freddie's lips. Freddie ran inside the plane with Dawson whooping it up after him.

Meanwhile, H.G. started a tantrum, and his whole entourage flew into hysterics. I hurried up the steps behind Janice Lang. In the excitement I still found time to enjoy the delightful view. Janice had stunning legs and a delicious anchorage.

Freddie and Dawson had disappeared into the john by the time I came into the plane. The plane was an old DC-4 that had been decorated by one of those Beverly Hills' fairies who have a thing for silks and satins and laces. It was like walking into Mae West's bedroom. The only thing lacking was the mirrors on the ceiling.

I walked up the aisle toward the front of the plane and spotted an empty seat next to Lisa Love. I quickly dropped into it.

"Anyone reserved this seat?"

"Yes."

"Who?"

"Me. I'm always allowed two seats. That way I can select my company."

I remained seated. "That's a fine idea."

"Yes, I think so." She was wearing a beige wool-knit outfit and a full-length mink coat. Her black hair was hidden under a white silk turban-type hat that was extremely becoming, making her thin sensitive face look even more delicate. "How is the protection racket these days?"

"Better than ever," I said. "H.G. promised me two things when I accepted this job. I've already received one, and right now I'm not too far away from the other. I understand H.G. is a man of his word."

"Where did you hear such garbage? That fat Jesus never does anything he promises."

"I'm sorry to hear that. Maybe, in this case, I can sort of nudge it along a bit. Give the old boy an assist."

"Well, if you want to join the rest of the ass-kissers ..."

"No, no," I said, smiling. "This I'm doing purely for my own selfish pleasure."

The stewardess closed the door, and from the window I saw the attendant pushing the ladder away from the plane, toward the entrance to the ramp. The first engine coughed and spat, smoke and flames shooting from its exhaust, and the whole plane shuddered, the strain singing in the metal. The stewardess came hurrying up the aisle, a worried frown on her face. Then I heard the commotion in the pilot's compartment and the door banged open.

"I can take it up," Dawson yelled. "There's nothing to it."

Freddie came out of the compartment, pulling Dawson by the shoulder.

"Please, sir, you must take your seats for the take-off," the stewardess said.

"Come here," Dawson said, grabbing the stewardess's arm. "Can I take your seat for a take-off?"

Her face turned a deep shade of pink as laughter erupted all over the plane.

"What's wrong with this jerk?" I asked.

"He's bored," Lisa said. "Just a bird-brain with more money than he knows what to do with."

I saw Freddie snap his fingers, and the Rock came rushing toward him. Dawson protested feebly while the Rock dragged him to a seat. All three sat down, and I lost sight of them.

After the take-off I glanced casually around the plane. Most of the claque was present. I saw Marsha, Tiny Tim, Phemie, Stone, Chauncey, Fowler, Jeff Strong and even Carolyn Montrose. There were other people I had never seen before, probably technical help. Lisa pointed out LeRoy Miller, the director of *Run for Home,* and George Marsh, the producer.

Except for an occasional yelp or howl from Freddie's corner, the first few hours of flight were unusually quiet and normal. Gus came by a couple times and chatted with us. Otherwise, Lisa and I sat mostly in silence, but it was a good silence, the kind that one usually enjoys only with a close friend. I closed my eyes and tried to nap, and I think I did for a few minutes. When I awoke, Lisa's head was resting on my shoulder and her eyes were closed. I reached over and placed my hand in hers, just letting it lie there in her warm lap.

"You're just a big farm boy, aren't you?" she said, without opening her eyes.

"Yes, ma'am."

"Holding hands is considered square."

"I don't care, ma'am. I've been hankering to do this a long time."

She opened one eye and smiled. "It's okay, sonny. If it makes you feel good inside, you just go ahead and be square."

"Yes, ma'am. There are other things, too, I'm hankering for."

"Yes, I can imagine."

"Don't you ever hanker, ma'am?"

"Constantly."

"Well, ma'am, maybe, we can hanker together."

"Maybe." She closed the eye again and gave my hand a little squeeze.

My blood surged up, nearly flooding my heart. We rested some more in silence. The laughter and talk was getting louder in Freddie's corner, and I was getting that uncomfortable feeling that something unpleasant was about to happen.

A moment later, Freddie's voice bellowed Chauncey's name, startling Lisa. She shook her head, her beautiful black eyes wide as she stared at me.

"Just Freddie clearing his throat," I said.

"Chauncey!" Freddie bellowed again.

"Oh, no," she said, her face clouding up. "Poor Chauncey."

Poor Chauncey dashed by me, his face set in a grim smile.

Dawson stood up and leaned against the back of the seat. "It's showtime, everybody. Come on, man, make like we're flying down to Rio."

There was a scattering of applause and Chauncey went into his act. He took more pratfalls, and gave them more variety in ten minutes than Red Skelton takes in a year. I started to worry for a while. Working in that narrow aisle began to look danger-ous, especially the way he was taking the falls. Freddie smiled, laughed once, then finally folded his arms across his chest and looked bored through it all. Dawson jumped up on the chair, sit-ting on top of the seat back, whooping it up, swinging a bottle of liquor in the air, sprinkling some of it on Chauncey's head whenever he got close enough to him.

Chauncey's face first turned red, then a deep purple. Perspiration ran down his face, soaking his shirt collar, and the little guy looked like he was going to have a stroke. My impulse was to dash up there and bang those two guys' heads together, but it was none of my business. If that was the way Chauncey chose to make a living, that was his business. Lisa stood next to me, unsmiling, her eyes almost completely shaded by her low-ered lids.

"It's disgusting," she said. "Like a monkey on a string. Why don't you make him stop?"

I placed my arm lightly across her shoulder. "It would only make it worse for Chauncey. The last thing he wants is pity."

"Oh, I know," she said. "But, dammit, why does he do it?"

I shook my head and tightened my grip around her, letting my arm drop to her waist.

Chauncey made a forward somersault and landed on his back. He stayed there, staring up at Freddie, face soaked, chest heaving, mouth open, panting hard.

"Come on," Dawson said. "Give us the back flip, man."

"I've got to rest," Chauncey gasped. "It's the altitude, I think."

"Cut the chatter, man. Let's go." Dawson jumped down from his seat and tried to raise Chauncey to his feet. "Let's go, now. I'm gonna butt you right in the ass. Come on. Get up, man. I'm getting mad."

Freddie was laughing again, pulling at his ear lobe, his porcelain caps sparkling. It was evident from his glazed eyes that he had done his share of drinking.

"Go on," Freddie said. "Kick him in the ass. It's all padded. Man, three inches of calluses. Might break your foot."

"Yeah, well, I'll kick him in the head then."

Chauncey got to his feet, his hands going to his heart, his head bowed. He was still having a hard time breathing.

"I'll be back," I said.

Both Freddie and Dawson were holding on to Chauncey when I got there. They were trying to flip him on his back.

"Break it up," I said, in my most austere cop tone.

Dawson staggered back a little when he tried to look up into my face. "Who's the creep?" he asked, turning to Freddie.

"Get lost, shamus," Freddie said. "This is none of your business."

I ignored the remarks. Dawson was closer and I grabbed him first, tearing him away from Chauncey in one violent motion. He came away, dancing on tiptoes. "Now, you sit down and behave or I'm liable to make you fly the rest of the way on your own power."

"F—" Dawson began the obscenity, but he never got a chance to finish it. I swung him around and shoved him into a seat so hard I thought the chair was coming apart.

I turned toward Freddie and found the Rock standing in front of him, waiting for me. Freddie was still holding on to Chauncey.

"Freddie," I said. "If I have to take this goon, it's going to cost you twenty grand in dental work once I finish with him. Now, either you go sit down like a good little man, or I'm going to bust you both wide open. And you, you ugly bastard, I owe you something." I unbuttoned my coat jacket and took one step toward the Rock, my hands balling up into hard fists.

"Break his back, Rock," Freddie said. "Go on, tear him to pieces."

The Rock stood his ground, and that was all right with me. I owed him something, and I always like to pay my debts. Suddenly, Milner jumped between us.

"Sweethearts," he cried. "Have you all lost your minds? We're all friends here. What's to fight about? Vince, don't do this."

Chauncey slowly dropped to his knees.

"Out of my way," I said, moving up to Chauncey. "Let go, Freddie. Chauncey, Chauncey, can you hear me? It's Slader. Is it your heart? Just nod if it is."

He nodded, and I gently stretched him out on the carpeted aisle. His forehead was cold and damp, his face greenish. He was actually strangling to death. His eyes slowly rolled back into his head, and for a moment I thought he was dead. The stewardess came up, but she didn't know what to do. I leaned down and started to breathe into his mouth. I stayed on my hands and knees, breathing like that, for over forty-five minutes before he started to breathe normally again. Then I carried him to a special lounge in the tail section of the plane and laid him out on a sofa, covering him with a blanket. He closed his eyes and fell sound asleep. The stewardess promised to stay with him.

Jeff Strong was sitting next to Lisa when I returned. I started to walk past, but Lisa stopped me.

"He's just leaving," she said, and Strong grinned, winking at me when he stood up. "Good show," he said, sauntering away.

"I just love movie people," I said.

"How is he?"

"Okay. It was a close one."

"You were marvelous."

"It's all relative. I just appear marvelous by comparison."

She leaned her head against my arm, and we both tried to sleep. We stopped somewhere for fuel, but I didn't even bother to look. No one was allowed to leave the plane. I slept after that, and when I awoke it was dark outside and the lights were on in the plane. Lisa was reading, her beautiful face covered by a huge pair of black horn-rimmed glasses. I looked at the book and did a double take. It was Proust's *Within a Budding Grove*. The propaganda in newspapers and magazines about the intellectual actor or actress who spent hours reading Proust and Dostoevski had always struck me as a little phony, to say the least. But she actually seemed to be reading it and, what's more, enjoying it. I was impressed.

I guess her peripheral vision was pretty good, because she closed the book and took off her glasses, tipping her head slightly to give me a sidelong glance.

"Have a good sleep?"

"Fine," I said, stretching a little. "It was just what the doctor ordered. Everything under control?"

"So, so. Freddie and Dirk are at it again. The Rock has been mixing drinks like mad."

"I suppose life gets to be quite a bore when you're rich and famous and you don't have any more brains than a magpie."

"Freddie's got brains, all right. So does Dirk. They're just neurotics."

At that moment, Freddie came strolling by with a glass in each hand.

"Wait for me," Dawson yelled, running up to him. "That's my drink you've got there, man. Fork it over."

Freddie laughed and faked a throw. Dawson screamed, ducking his head under his arms. "Man, that's too good to waste. Come on, give me a little sip."

Freddie laughed and handed him a glass. "Here's to Slader, the fearless dick," Dawson said, tipping up the glass and emptying it in one huge gulp.

Suddenly he stiffened, his arms straightening out, his eyes bulging out of his head, his head going back as he gasped for breath. The next thing I knew, he was dancing around, bumping against the seats, his mouth wide open, screaming without a sound. I thought he was clowning until I saw the tiny puffs of smoke coming from his gaping mouth. Then I looked down at the floor, where the glass had fallen, and saw the widening hole in the carpeting.

"Get some milk, somebody," I cried, trying to grab Dawson, who by now was jumping three feet off the floor, flailing his arms about wildly, still unable to make a sound. I didn't have to get too close to his mouth to get a whiff of that acid. Tiny Tim handed me a glass of water, and I dumped it on the floor.

"Milk, I told you," I said, pushing him away. But by the time the milk arrived Dawson had passed out.

Freddie trembled as he stared down at Dawson's agonized, twisted body, a look of horror stamped across his face, the muscles along his jawline twitching. "Who did it?" he cried. Then he looked at the glass in his own hand and dropped it, jumping away from it as it splashed. I reached down and touched the liquid. It was just plain whisky. We looked at each other and Freddie knew what I was thinking. Attempt number two to murder Freddie Sharpe had failed.

"Who gave me that glass?" he demanded, his voice breaking, close to panic.

"He did it," Phemie White accused in a shrill hysterical voice, shaking a long finger at the Rock. "I saw him. He's the one."

Freddie spun around, his face twisting furiously. "You dirty sonofabitch," he screamed, running toward the Rock. I stepped in front of him. "I'll handle it," I said.

"He tried to kill me," Freddie cried. "That sonofabitch. After all I've done for him. Give me your gun, Slader. I'm gonna kill him myself."

The Rock hadn't moved, but his eyes were darting around wildly, his hands clenching nervously at his side. "I didn't do it," he protested. "It wasn't me. I swear it."

"Kill him," Freddie said. "Give me your gun. I'll do it right now."

"Nobody's going to kill anybody right now. Come over here, Rock."

"No," he said, backing away, his hand reaching out for a whisky bottle. "I didn't do it."

"Then come here. You've got nothing to worry about."

Freddie reached down and picked up the empty glass, hurling it at the Rock, striking him on the shoulder.

The Rock howled in anger and rushed toward us, brandishing the bottle in mid-air. I brushed Freddie quickly aside and stepped forward to meet the Rock's drive. There was more than a personal score to settle now. This was a crazy man, a man gone berserk with fear and anger. A man on the kill.

The jaw hardened, and the eyes disappeared in the contorted face. "Bastards," he roared, swinging the bottle for the top of my head.

There wasn't much room for maneuver in that narrow aisle. All I could do was duck my head and charge. The bottle exploded halfway down my back. At that same instant my head banged into his chest, knocking him back, blasting the wind out of him. I tried to straighten up and I couldn't. My back felt like an ax had plunged into it, severing my spine. I saw his knee come up into my face and I couldn't even move out of the way. It exploded against my cheekbone and lights burst in my head. I went down to my knees, my arms grappling for a hold around his legs. I could hear the wild screaming around me, and above it all was Freddie's voice, screeching for the kill. I was fighting blindly now, without thought or reason, and with less than half my strength. All that kept going through my mind was the crazy idea that he was going to take me. The Rock was going to beat my brains in, and I was going to lie there at his feet and take it.

I have been in a lot of tough situations, but at the moment I couldn't think of a worse one. All this happened in split seconds. My fingers twisted on the back of his legs, digging into the hard muscles just above the knees, and I held on, pulling him toward me with all my strength. He hit me with three or four rabbit punches before going down. But he went down, and I struggled to get on top of him. We rolled down the aisle, bumping against the chairs on both sides.

We fought in silence, grunting and groaning, struggling desperately for an advantage. For a moment I was on top of him, and I threw a short hard right that splashed against his nose, slamming his head against the floor. I followed it up with half a dozen chopping jabs before he slipped away from under me and jumped to his feet. I jumped right after him and nearly passed out from the pain in my back. He charged in fast, head down, huge fists lashing out viciously, driving me back by the sheer fury and precision of the attack. We went all the way down the aisle that way, until my back struck the closed door leading to the pilot's compartment. He closed in quickly, his hard fists pounding into my stomach and chest. He was grinning now, sure of victory, his breath coming in short, harsh puffs.

We stood toe to toe, swinging at each other, until my arms felt leaden and my body swollen tight with pain. Then suddenly I shifted to my right, hitting him in the throat with the flat edge of my left hand. He stumbled toward the door, and for an instant his guard went down, leaving his face open for the left hook that piled into it. I put what remained of my shoulder and body into that punch. It slammed into the big jaw like a pile driver, shattering it like a delicate crystal goblet. He cried out, a surprised look on his face, and fell against the door, his knees buckling under him.

I stepped back and turned away. Somebody screamed and I spun around, not knowing what to expect.

I was too late.

The gun nearly exploded in my face.

I threw myself down, my hand automatically going for my gun. My heart was pounding so loud I was sure everybody could hear it. Perspiration flooded down my forehead and swam into my eyes, smarting and blurring my vision. I saw the Rock, still leaning against the door, one leg folded under his sagging body, the gun wavering in his hand as he tried to aim it at me. The gun seemed very heavy in his hand, and I cursed myself for having turned my back on him, for not having finished him off with a solid right. I had been stupid, and now I was going to have to pay for it. Maybe with my life.

My fingers were clutching the .38 special, ripping it out of the holster, when the Rock's gun barked at me again, spitting fire and lead in my direction. My whole body froze for the single tick of a clock, and I heard the slug slam into the floor about two feet in back of my head. My own gun had cleared the holster, and I started to roll on my side, wanting to be ready to aim the instant the gun was clear and in the open.

The Rock was trying to stand up, his broken jaw hanging limply to one side, his dark eyes full of pain and murder. The gun burst into flame again, and the slug smashed into the metal base of a chair to my right and ricocheted with a ping, ping, ping, all the way up the aisle.

The shooting sequence took place in a matter of split seconds that seemed like hours. I never thought I'd ever get that damn gun out, but I did, my finger gently squeezing the hair trigger in spite of the panic. The gun throbbed in my fist just once. The Rock cried out, a look of astonishment spreading across his face. Suddenly, he was standing up, walking toward me, his big hands up above his head, the gun hooked to his index finger, his broken jaw flapping grotesquely, his eyes wide and full of horror.

I could hear everybody on the plane sucking for breath, and I scrambled to my feet. Suddenly, his legs melted under him and he fell headlong, like a dead man, without the slightest effort to brace himself.

17

Herman Erickson had been chief of police in Elkwood, Kansas, for over forty years. He made that particular point forty times in the first forty minutes.

In the forty years that Herman Erickson had been chief of police, nothing like this had ever happened in Elkwood, Kansas. But the more he talked, the more impressed I became with the idea that he was grateful to us for having brought our troubles to his door.

"You don't have to worry about a thing, gentlemen," he said, puffing on his cigar behind his polished desk. "My men will take care of everything."

Unfortunately, there wasn't anything for his men to take care of. The Rock was in the hospital with a slug in his abdomen. Dirk Dawson was in the hospital with a severe case of acid burns and poisoning. And Chauncey was in the hospital for a rest and a complete examination. The case, as far as I was concerned, was closed. The Rock was our man, and from what the doctors said his chance of ever going to trial was slim.

We landed at Elkwood just half an hour after the shooting. The municipal airport had been all lighted up, and the high-school band had marched up to the plane, playing some of Freddie's top hits. In a town of about thirty thousand, over fifty thousand had been at the airport to greet Freddie. The pilot had radioed ahead for an ambulance, but even the sight of the ambulance and the men being carried out on the stretchers had not dimmed the crowd's enthusiasm. Phalanxes of high-school girls lined the roped areas, waving banners and placards, squealing hysterically when he stepped out of the plane. Freddie waved, muttering obscenities under his breath, smiling in a sober, charming way. The crowd really went wild when he got into the ambulance and rode away to the hospital with his friend, Dirk Dawson.

Lisa Love and Jeff Strong also created excitement when they came out, but the crowd soon lost interest when the ambulance disappeared down the ramp.

Gus Milner and I rode to police headquarters with Chief Erickson.

"Too bad about all this," the chief said. "We had a nice reception all lined up. We'd been planning this for a long time. This was to be a great occasion for Elkwood."

"It still can be," Gus said. "Listen, Chief, we're still shooting here tomorrow. Nothing has been changed. In fact, we're glad this has happened." Gus then proceeded to give a long-winded review of the whole case, from the threatening notes to the brake line and finally to the acid on the plane. The chief nodded at all the right spots, his small, round eyes appreciative of Gus's confidences.

When Gus finished, the chief pulled the cigar out of his mouth and looked at me, smiling like a pleased uncle about to pat a nephew on the head. "Mr. Slader, that was a mighty fine act of heroism. In wartime, you would have received the Silver Star for such an action. Maybe, even the Congressional Medal of Honor. Who knows?"

Politicans are always alike. Elkwood or L.A. or New York. It's all the same. It's like they all came out of the same vat. They're all one color.

"Gus," I said. "Maybe we can find a little spot for Chief Erickson in *Run for Home*. Be a big help to him come next election."

"Well," the chief said, nervously flipping ashes on his polished desk, "you don't have to do that. But if you've got a little part for me, I'd be glad to do it without any charge whatsoever. As long, of course, as it's right for me. It would have to be something with dignity. Maybe I could play a public official. Something along that order. I hope you understand. Don't take me wrong. I know that good people play bad parts in the movies. It has nothing to do with their character. But, you see, with me it's different. I couldn't play the part of a gangster or crooked official. That might tend to create a wrong impression in the public's mind."

By this time Gus was waving for the chief to stop. "I know, I know," he said. "I follow you a hundred per cent. We'll get you a swell role, even if we have to write one in for you. Believe me, chief. We're on your side. All we ask in return is for you to keep law and order. We can't very well shoot this film with people breaking into our sets. Some scenes we'll want to shoot right here downtown, and we'll need your help to close off the streets, and so forth. You understand?"

"I most certainly do. You can depend on me. I've already talked with some of the men from Goldman Studios, and I will do my best to help in any way possible. Please call on me any time."

Finally we left and took a cab to Freddie's rented house. It was the most lavish house in Elkwood, belonging to a contractor who was presently vacationing in Europe. Lisa's house was directly across the street. It was a smaller house, and older, but I doubted that it bothered Lisa very much.

"Well, Gus," I said, after he had toured the house to make sure everything was ready for Freddie when he returned from the hospital. "It's time for me to check out. I plan on taking the first plane back to L.A."

"Sweetheart, you're kidding."

"The case is closed. I'm just a fifth wheel now."

"But you're not. Listen, sweetheart, we need somebody to guard Freddie."

"From what?"

"Vince, Vince, Vince. Freddie is an idol. Don't you know what that means? Why, listen, Freddie can't even walk down the street without some bastard trying to knock him down. Listen, this boy goes into a bar, any bar, I don't care where, and some drunk wants to knock his teeth down his throat. This man, who is loved by millions, leads the life of public enemy number one. I mean it. He needs protection twenty-four hours a day. Being a celebrity is a great responsibility and an even greater burden. The man carries a cross through life. And the bigger he becomes, the heavier the cross. Sometimes, I know, he wishes he could chuck the whole thing down the drain. And I don't blame him. I would be tempted myself. I mean it, Vince. I don't think I could stand it. It's a terrible strain on one's nervous system. No wonder so many entertainers go nuts. Can you blame them? The pressure is fantastic. It comes from all sides and slowly crushes you like a—like a—you know, one of those things you wind up."

"Vise?"

"Right, vise. And, man, they really turn that screw. Sweetheart, believe me, I'm satisfied just where I am. And you should be, too. Freddie can keep it. He deserves all he can get. Good luck to him. God bless him. And all that stuff. I don't envy him one moment. And don't you envy him, either. You pay for what you get in this world. And don't worry, Freddie is paying plenty. Look at today. His best friend almost murdered before his eyes. And then to realize that it was intended for him. If that boy doesn't crack up now, he never will. He's tough. You've got to give him credit. The man is tough. He was born in Brooklyn, you know, on a real tough street. I guess he learned a lot there. He's got concrete inside of him—" and Gus tapped his chest—"when he needs it. And, other times, you've never seen a more softhearted, generous man. I mean it, sweetheart. This boy will give you the very shirt right off his back if he likes you. But if he doesn't like you, you can drop dead in front of him and he'll spit on your head. That's the kind of a man he is. He works hard and plays just as hard. Earns big. Spends big."

I had walked over to a leather-upholstered bar in a corner of the living room to mix myself a drink while he was talking. My back was still in pretty bad shape, among other things, and all I could think about was a steaming hot shower. I also didn't want to get hooked on any bodyguard deal.

"Gus," I said, interrupting him. "Don't bother. I can't take the job. You can buy muscles for a hundred bucks a week. Why pay me a thousand?"

"Okay," he said. "Just one or two days until we can fly the Killer out here. Will you do that for me? Please, Vince. And I won't ask you for another thing. I promise."

"Two days is the maximum," I said. "After that, Killer or no Killer, I'm leaving."

"It's a deal."

We shook hands and I went to take that shower.

That evening they all met in the living room for a story conference. There was Freddie, Gus, Lisa, Janice, Jeff, Phemie, Carl, LeRoy Miller and George Marsh.

I stayed in the background and consumed four or five drinks. Finally I stretched out on a sofa and tried to shut out the voices. There was nothing going on there I particularly wanted to hear. All the talk was about the picture and how they were going to film certain scenes. Miller, the director, seemed the most articulate. No matter what anybody said, he would pick it up and shape it into an image for the camera. He was young, not more than thirty, and noted for his brilliance in television. This was to be his first movie. He had a New York theatrical accent that grated on my nerves. Soon I closed my eyes and fell into a deep sleep.

I think it was a voice that first woke me up. I'm not sure. If it was, it happened almost simultaneously with the explosion of the gun. I jumped clear off the sofa, landing flat-footed, shoulders hunched over like a fullback waiting for the snap of the ball.

Freddie stood about twenty feet away, a gun in one hand and a drink in the other. He was laughing. I knew without even touching my holster that the gun pointed at my head was my own .38 special.

"Hey, shamus, how did you do that today? You know, that Marshal Dillon bit. Was it like this?" He laughed and pulled the trigger. The slug plowed into the sofa not more than six inches from my leg.

This guy either had something in mind or he was a lunatic. Either way, it didn't look too healthy for me.

"What are you trying to prove, Freddie?" I said, glancing around the room for the first time. I saw Gus holding on to Lisa, both of them as far away from Freddie as they could get.

"I don't know yet, shamus. I'll think of something. You know, you're not the only cat who can handle a rod. Man, I was brought up with one of them things. I had a rod when I was twelve. Listen, shamus, where I come from you had to be tough to survive. I knew all the tough guys, and the smart ones, too. I know all about that jazz. I've been around, man. I know guys like Luciano. Good friend of mine. What do you think of that?"

"I'm impressed. Now give me the gun." I took a couple of steps toward him.

"Stop! You move when I tell you." He giggled and emptied his drink, yelling to Gus for a refill. "I think I'm gonna drill you, shamus. Maybe in the leg. I don't know yet." Gus brought him a fresh drink, and hurried back to Lisa's side.

"Gus is scared of me. How you like that, shamus? You scared of me, too? Are you?"

"I don't know yet," I said. "I'll let you know in a few minutes."

"Gotta think it over, eh?" The gun went off again, the slug digging into the floor just in front of my feet. "I'll bet I could put one right between your eyes if I wanted to."

"Sure," I said. "And you could join your pal Joey in Death Row."

OVID DEMARIS

"Joey was a crum. My pals are big men."

"I've thought it over," I said. "Either you shoot me or put the gun down. I'm coming to get it and I'm going to do it the hard way, big man."

"You stay put until I tell you to move. I mean it."

"Shoot it or drop it," I said, starting toward him, trying to hold his eyes with a hard stare.

He fired again, this time above my head. I kept coming. I had him figured. He was still the poor, skinny beanpole who had sucked around the big punks on the block back in Brooklyn. He hadn't had any guts then and he didn't have any now.

I was about six feet away when he threw the gun at me. The hammer was in a firing position and about as dangerous as a coiled rattler about to strike. My hand came out to snatch it from the air and then pulled back instinctively. I let it fly past me, throwing myself to the floor, yelling for Gus and Lisa to do the same. We all hit the floor at about the same time the gun went off. A lamp where Gus had been a moment before shattered into a hundred pieces. I stood up and retrieved the gun. Then I walked up to Freddie and, without saying a word, slammed him hard on each side of the face. His eyes blinked and tears of pain ran down his cheeks.

Lisa caught up with me on the front steps.

"Where are you going in the middle of the night?" she asked, taking my hand and squeezing it.

"Away from here," I said.

"Come with me," she said. "I'll put you up for the night."

I followed her across the street and into the house.

"Would you like a drink?"

"Yes," I said. "Straight bourbon, if you have any."

She looked drawn and tired, and to me, all the more beautiful. I was surprised at how little make-up she used. She handed me the drink and I pulled her down on the sofa next to me.

"I'm leaving in the morning," I said. "And I may never see you again."

146

"Yes," she said. "I've been thinking about that."

"You're beautiful."

"Thank you."

"You're the most beautiful woman I've ever seen."

"You want to kiss me?"

"More than anything," I said, pulling her against me, my lips finding her sweet mouth. I held on to her a long time, my hands caressing the smooth planes of her back. Her hands pulled my head down against her shoulder, and I kissed her soft white throat.

"Do you want me?" she whispered, her breath warm and exciting in my ear.

In answer, I stood up and swept her into my arms. "Where's the bedroom?" I said, kissing her open mouth as she tried to answer.

I gently lowered her onto the bed, kneeling beside her, my head resting on her soft warm breasts. Her hands slipped inside my jacket and moved across my chest and under my arms, then up to the back of my neck, squeezing it with her long slim fingers.

"Take my clothes off," she whispered. "And I'll take yours off."

Her breathing got heavier, but neither one of us spoke, afraid to break the spell. Then we lay on the bed and tenderly explored the strange, mysterious areas of each other's bodies.

I raised up on one elbow and kissed each erect breast, my hand marveling at the velvet smoothness of her thighs.

I felt her hand on me, searching, and I moved in closer. I watched her eyes as her hand closed on me, and I buried my mouth into hers, crushing my lips against her teeth, hungry for the hot piercing tongue that darted against my lips.

"Now," she cried. "Please, hurry, now. Oh, now!"

And it was *now*. And then later it was *now* again. It was *now* throughout the night.

W E BOTH slept in the morning until the maid tiptoed into the room and gently rocked me back to consciousness.

"There's a telephone call for you, sir. A Sergeant Delaney."

I jumped out of bed, looking frantically around the room for the telephone. When I realized I was in the raw, I already had the phone in my hand.

"Sorry," I said, trying to cross my legs with dignity.

She didn't crack a smile or bat an eyelash. "I understand, sir."

I was glad, because she wasn't a day older than twenty-one.

She went out, gently closing the door, and I sat on the edge of the bed, near Lisa.

"I thought you were going to call me," Frank said. He sounded a little peeved.

"Frank, forgive me—everything happened so fast around here, I completely forgot. I'm sorry."

"What's this I read about the Rock?"

"He's the one," I said. "Fat fingerprints and all."

"No, he's not," Frank said. "You've got the wrong boy."

"I've what?"

"The Killer is your man. At least, it was his prints on the creeper."

"That could be wrong. Maybe, he was just helping Juan around the garage."

"Good try, but not good enough. We've already picked up the Killer, and I have a nice little confession with his signature appended to the bottom thereof."

"Maybe they were working together?"

"No dice. He got the idea all by himself. This boy has a mean temper, and when Freddie hired you he thought he was getting the boot. The Lewis notes gave him the idea. He was in this all by himself."

"Thanks, Frank. That makes everything about as clear as mud."

"I don't know what you've got yourself up there. But it sounds like a bear with a short tail."

"That it is," I said. "And I'm just about to let go."

"Good luck. Send me a post card."

"I said good-by and just sat there with the dead phone in my hand.

"Trouble?" Lisa said.

"Much trouble," I said.

"Can I help?"

"Maybe," I said. "How about doing it over a cup of coffee?"

Plenty of crazy, wild thoughts went through my head as I hurriedly dressed. Something had gone wrong, somewhere, and I couldn't put my finger on it.

The coffee arrived, and I brought a chair up to the bed. Lisa propped a pillow under her head and pulled the pink sheet above her breasts. She sipped at the coffee while I brought her up to date on the crazy, mixed-up caper.

"Now," I said, concluding. "I think the Rock was just an innocent bystander. I can't find the slightest motive for his trying to kill Freddie."

"Maybe he was trying to kill Dawson."

"No. That's not it. And besides, the Rock had been mixing the drinks. It would have been a bonehead play all around."

"It does sound stupid."

"There's something I'm missing here. I can feel it. There have been two distinct and separate attempts to murder Freddie. The first one is taken care of. The Killer had a motive, and the idea came from Lewis. All right, now both these people are back in L.A. The contusing thing is that there is no connecting thread. It looks like the same idea struck a number of people at the same time." I stopped and tasted the coffee.

"I'm fascinated," she said. "I know it's gruesome and all that, but it's still fascinating."

"Listen," I said. "How did the Rock end up holding the bag on this deal? Things happened so quickly there for a minute, I can't remember. The first thing I knew Freddie was yelling and the Rock was coming at me with a bottle."

"Wait a minute," she said, sitting up straight, the sheet dropping from her gorgeous breasts. "It was Phemie. She's the one who saw him do it."

That was all I needed to know. I kisssed her with gratitude and a good deal of affection, maybe even a little passion.

Phemie had a suite at the local Biltmore. It was about nine-thirty when I rang the bell. The first thing I saw when the door opened was the cigarette holder and the arm full of bangles.

"Oh, it's you," she said.

"It's me," I said, pushing my way in. "I hope it's not before breakfast time."

"It is," she said, walking away from me, giving me a full view of the dragon on the back of her kimono. "Well, what is it now? Make it brief. I have to be on the set by ten."

"How long it takes depends on you," I said, sitting on the arm of a fat chair. "I would like for you to help me trace the action leading up to the shooting on the plane yesterday."

"Why me?"

"Well, for one thing, it was you who accused the Rock of putting the acid in the drink."

She kept her back turned to me, but I could see her neck stiffen. "Me? I did no such thing. What are you trying to do?"

"Phemie," I said. "You just made a very serious mistake."

"Oh? I don't see what you mean."

"Turn around and look at me."

"I'm perfectly comfortable the way I am."

"It doesn't matter, Phemie. You know, for an actress and dramatic coach, you've got a lot to learn about real acting. I've met hoods who had never taken a lesson in their lives who could teach you plenty."

"I am not acting," she said. "I don't like you, Slader, and I want you to go."

"Phemie, when I go, you're coming with me. Being a gambling man, I'm willing right now to bet my reputation that you were the one who put the acid in Freddie's glass."

The holder dropped from her stiff fingers, but she still kept her back turned to me. "You're insane," she said. "What ghastly reason would I have to do such a morbid thing?"

"The best reason in the world, besides money. Love! You saw what Freddie did to Adela and you planned your own brand of ironic justice. The fire destroyed her beauty, and the acid was supposed to destroy the one thing that is beautiful in Freddie. His voice. This is a woman's weapon, Phemie. It is not the type of weapon a guy like the Rock would use. Maybe, if you had kept your mouth shut, you might have gotten away with it. Who knows?"

My gaze had wandered away from her while I talked. Suddenly, she let out a sharp, wounded cry and turned. "I'll kill you," she cried, hurling herself at me, her long fingers and pointed nails aimed at my face.

I didn't want to hurt her, but I didn't want those claws on my face, either. I was sitting on the arm of the chair, and I fell into it, scooting down and away from her. She caught a handful of hair and scratched me in the face and neck a good dozen times before I could get a hold of her hands. That dame didn't pack much weight, but she was all tigress under that parched skin.

She cried after that, her thin narrow shoulders jumping with the sobs, her flat chest quivering with each gasping breath.

It took Chief Erickson's men less than five minutes to answer the call. I guess the Chief was really serious about that movie part.

I took a cab to the hospital. The least I could do was to apologize to the Rock. The Rock had acted foolishly, but he was an innocent man, and I don't like to leave things like that undone.

The hospital was a small two-story white building, perched on top of a rolling green hill. I introduced myself to the receptionist and, after communicating with Chief Erickson, she escorted me up a long, extremely antiseptic corridor. The uniformed cop stood up from his white stool and moved in front of the door.

"It's all right, Ralph," the girl said. "Chief Erickson has given his approval."

"Okay, Arline," he said, going back to his stool.

I thanked Arline and went in, quickly closing the door before she could follow me in. What I had to say was better said in privacy.

The bed was empty. The room was empty. The Rock was nowhere around. The window was open and I walked to it, looking down at the soft green grass one story below.

I waited a couple of minutes before leaving, not wanting to arouse the guard's suspicion. He didn't even look at me when I left.

My cab was still waiting, and I told him to make tracks for Freddie's house.

I took the front steps four at a time and raced through the entry hall, coming to a breathless halt in the center of the living room. There was a dead silence in the house that bristled the hairs on the back of my neck. I didn't waste time thinking about it. Freddie's bedroom was the last one down the long hallway. I stopped before the closed door and turned the knob slowly. The drapes were drawn and the room was in semidarkness. I caught sight of two shadows at the far end of the room and my hand crept to the holster at my side.

Freddie was standing beside the large bed, his back curved over a night stand, his hands held up protectively before his chest, his eyes wide and transfixed on the long, thick butcher knife in the Rock's hand. The Rock stood no more than three feet away from him, leaning forward like a man with a bad stomach pain, the knife held close to his body. The Rock's head had been wrapped in white bandages to support his wired jaw.

Neither one spoke nor moved. There was an unreal quality to the picture, like a movie reel stuck on a single frame, with all motion arrested.

"Hold it right there," I called, aiming the .38 special at his bandaged head.

The words startled them both as though out of a weird dream. The Rock jumped back, his body turning painfully toward me. He started to nod the moment he recognized me, the knife coming up in a menacing gesture as he stumbled toward me, one hand pressed against his stomach.

I let him come, one wobbly step after another, like a man walking a tightrope in a high wind. The important thing was to get him away from within striking distanc eof Freddie.

When he had covered about ten feet, I called a halt. "That's far enough," I said, bracing my legs. "Now drop the knife."

He shook his huge head angrily and came on. From the corner of my eye, I saw Freddie's hand dip into the night stand drawer, and before I could yell for him to stop, the gun exploded.

The Rock spun around, lunging toward Freddie.

"Don't!" I screamed.

The gun barked again. I guess the slug must have struck solid bone this time, because the impact lifted the Rock's feet right off the floor, slapping him down on his seat. He sat there, stunned, a great roar escaping through his clenched teeth, then gently slid sideways. He was dead before his head hit the floor.

Milner rushed into the room, his gray face twisted with terror. He stopped when he saw the gun in my hand, and for a moment he couldn't utter a sound. He just pointed at the Rock.

"He's dead," I said, turning to glare at Freddie. "Freddie just murdered him."

Freddie swore, waving the gun in my direction. "You're crazy. It was self-defense, and you know it. You saw the knife. You saw him try to kill me. What are you trying to pull?"

"You better put that gun down," I said. "Or I might have to plug you in self-defense."

He looked down at the gun in his hand, then at the gun in my hand, aimed squarely at his guts, and suddenly smiled, giving me the full porcelain treatment. "What are we fighting about?" he said, casually tossing the gun on the bed. "I've got a right to protect myself in my home. After all the guy tried to kill me once before."

"This is the Rock," I said. "This lump of garbage at your feet is Rocco Scarpianno, your first cousin, and your personal stooge for ten years. Doesn't that mean anything to you?"

"Sure it means something." He stopped and glanced at the corpse, moving back slightly. "I'm sorry he's dead. But I had no choice. He tried to kill me twice."

"Just once," I said. "And I don't think he would have done it."

"What do you mean by that?"

"I've got a few things to say to you, Freddie, and you better listen for once in your life. It wasn't the Rock who put the acid in your glass. It was Phemie." Then I quickly outlined the whole messy situation for him, going back to the Lewis notes and the Killer. When I finished Gus was wringing his hands, and there was a frozen expression on Freddie's face.

He shook his head, rubbing his neck. "I don't get it. I just don't get it. I really don't get any of it."

I even thought of explaining it to him, but what good would it have done? This guy believed only what he wanted to believe. I slipped the gun back into the holster and buttoned my jacket.

"See you around, Freddie," I said.

"Wait. Where are you going? I need you. If what you say is true, how do I know somebody else won't try it?"

"You don't," I said. "That's the beauty of being popular."

"Now, wait. I need protection."

"There's no protection for you, Freddie. The only way you can be safe is by locking yourself in a vault and swallowing the key."

"Stay, Slader. I'll pay you anything you want."

"Good-by, Freddie. Good luck, Gus." I turned on my heels and started out of the room.

"Go, you sonofabitch," Freddie screamed. "Who needs you? You dirty, lousy, goddam shamus. I'll have Nick take care of you. You wait and see."

Sure, Freddie, I thought. Have Nick take care of me. But who's going to take care of you? Who's going to protect you from your claque? From your unholy claque?

"Go, you bastard. Go! Go! Go! I don't need nobody." I heard his footsteps behind me all the way down the long hallway and into the living room. "I'm Freddie Sharpe," he screamed. "I'm the only one I need. Go on, get out of here, you lousy bum! Run into your hole!"

I turned back for a fleeting glance. He stood before the huge fireplace, his dark face full of hate, waving his long slender hands like a dictator on a balcony.

"I can buy guys like you at a dime a dozen. You're cheap, shamus. Real dirt cheap!"

I heard the timid, frightened voice of Gus in the background, trying to calm him down. "Please, sweetheart, don't excite yourself. It's okay. We'll get somebody else. Everything will be all right."

"Listen, that goes for you, too, you crummy little bloodsucker. If you want to go—go. Go on, follow Slader. Get out! Who gives a damn? I don't need nobody. Understand? Nobody!"

"Now, now, sweetheart, I don't want to go. I'm your pal. I'd do anything for you."

"Janice! Janice! Where the hell is she? I want Janice."

"She's on the set."

"On the set? For Christ's sake, get me somebody. Go on, move."

"There's Carolyn Montrose."

"Who?"

"The redhead…"

"Get her. Go on, shake it up! Move, goddammit!"

The last sound I heard was Gus' plaintive cry, scratching at the sonic barrier, inviting Carolyn to her destiny.

www.ingramcontent.com/pod-product-compliance
Lightning Source LLC
Chambersburg PA
CBHW052008240626
47153CB00008B/2791